RED- THE NEW RULEBOOK & PETE ZENDEL SERIES (BOOK 1)

BY USA TODAY BESTSELLING AUTHOR

JOY OHAGWU

LifeFountainMedia

CONTENTS

SCRIPTURE

Foundational Scripture

~

"I am the Way, and the Truth, and the Life: no one comes to the Father but through Me." **JESUS** (John 14:6)

ACKNOWLEDGMENTS

~

It's not every day one begins writing a book and is able to finish it. I, for one, couldn't have completed The New Rulebook without the help and support of the following. First and foremost, thank you, Lord Jesus Christ—my Lord, Savior, Master, Keeper, and best friend—for this story! May every word glorify you. Thank you Holy Spirit, for the inspiration and impromptu worship sessions that resulted during the writing process! Great times in your presence—one I pray continues.

Thank you, Mom, for believing in my dreams and for first showing me love involves sacrifice. I'm blessed to have you as my Mom! You remain our family's professor, and I learn from you always. Thank you, Precious, my little sister, for playing family chef when

I was too engrossed in creating this story to observe the difference between an apple and a potato.
Uncle Bonny, Aunty Linda, and Uncle Sam, thank you for everything you have all done for me in times past. May God bless and reward you richly.
Deirdre Lockhart, of Brilliant Cut Editing, the day I won your Valentine's Day contest this year was a double blessing. Our collaboration has been fun, tempered with humor yet much of the time, focused. Meeting you and working with you has been such a rewarding experience. This wouldn't be the polished product it is today without your expert guidance. I'm very grateful to you and proud of what we've accomplished!
To my readers, thank you for choosing my book! Let's continue this journey together.

Joy Ohagwu, August 2014.

DESCRIPTION

Gripped by shock at the site of a presumed routine package delivery run, business woman and entrepreneur Ruby "Red" Masters just saw a woman die. And she discovered The New Rulebook, something she knew nothing about. But it knew everything about her, enough to frame her for murder. As the clock ticks, Ruby calls on the one person she trusts, her best friend and police officer, Robert Towers. Robert will find a way out. He always has.

But as they race against time and beyond the reach of an unknown enemy, Ruby didn't count on Robert falling in love with her--and turning Christian. Robert's unrelenting grip on his newfound faith irritates Ruby, until she's captured behind enemy lines. When all human effort fails her, will she find that what she needed was right there all along? Or will she rebuff the love of the God she doesn't see, and that of the man she'd always known as simply a friend?

RED is Book 1 in The New Rulebook & Pete Zendel Christian Suspense Series, a #1 bestselling & award winning series in Christian Romantic Suspense.

Praise for RED:

"Ohagwu's tale interlocks suspense and romance. Delightful Christian Suspense." Readers' Favorite

"A 5-star for sure."- Amazon Reviewer

"...wholesome christian stories that pack the same engrossing punch as secular books but without the offensive content." - Amazon Reviewer

"If you like clean christian suspense, this book is for you." - Amazon Reviewer

"This mystery is well written and keeps you on the edge of your reading chair. They characters are well developed and believable."- Amazon Reviewer

"If you've faced crossroads in your life and faith, you might especially enjoy this action adventure story."- Amazon Reviewer

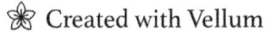

To JESUS: WHO alone is love personified

1

...*THERE IS A TIME FOR EVERY EVENT UNDER HEAVEN.*
Ecclesiastes 3:1

"Why don't you shoot me first?"

Her brown eyes pierced mine with disturbing certainty. She was maybe five feet five inches tall, and I'd guess Hispanic if I had to. She was clad in a simple formal outfit and could pass for any pedestrian. Except she wasn't, because someone paid me a fortune to meet her here. She wove her right palm around her left one, her thin, dry lips parting slightly as she inhaled a deep breath while casting a nervous glance around us. She turned her back to me, and the gravel crunched along with every step she took.

Staring at her well-groomed, short, and curly hair,

I steadied my nerves. The side glass-walled pane of the unoccupied high-rise building partially mirrored her square-shaped face when she stopped mere inches from the structure.

I closed the gap as I noticed that the rising sun behind me cast a curved shadow to the left, obscuring my view of the cordoned-off parking lot I'd passed only minutes earlier. Construction crews worked quite some distance away. In contrast to their grating noise, her still frame exuded an unsettling composure —one that was much too calm. A wave of strong springtime winds rushed by, rustling freshly-bloomed red petals of an unkempt poppy patch nearby, while demurely revealing the neckline of her white-collared shirt.

I opened my mouth, but no words came. I set my purse on the ground and warded off the alarm bells going off in my mind. I rolled down my jacket sleeves. *Just keep this interaction professional.* I cleared my throat aloud.

"Excuse me, my name is Ruby Masters. I run a freelance delivery service. Cortexe Corp.—which I believe you work for—paid me to show up here to meet you. Probably to confirm your arrival with a package for me, but I'm not sure." I pulled out my clipboard and waited for her to interject. She didn't, so I continued, "Can I please have the package for delivery? I, for one, I'm certainly not here to kill anyone." I let out a short nervous laugh and waited for her to take my cue and say something—*anything.* Still, she was silent.

Maybe she never even heard me. *Okay, time to call it a day.* With a wave, I brushed my hair back, pulling it into a tight bun. Zipping up my purse halfway, I saw her feet move as she turned around. So I straightened to meet her gaze.

"They see everything." She looked me in the eye, unwavering, her voice even calmer than the first time she spoke, her jaw tipping slightly upward with an air of sophistication. She waved her hand in the air, a stiff smile crossing her face. "In the restaurants, I mean —*everything.*" She continued looking into my eyes and yet didn't blink once.

"I built The New Rulebook," she emphasized every word.

I frowned a little. "You mean, like surveillance, like what the government—"

She shook her head so fast, short curls bounced over her forehead. But she kept her eyes on me as she reached inside her sweater, pulled out an object, and handed it to me.

I accepted it without breaking eye contact.

"No, not like that," she responded. "What the government has now is...old, very old compared to The New Rulebook. That's the name of what I built. Nothing is hidden from it—*nothing.* Only glitch is one-tenth of it isn't there." She turned toward the now-familiar blank spot on her wall of the high-rise building.

I secured what she gave me, placing it in the inside pocket of my leather jacket and zipping up without investigating the contents. I could do so later. First, I needed to understand who this woman was and what we were doing here. What was my job if not purely delivery service? "What am I supposed to—"

The *whoosh* of an object blew past the left side of my head from behind, grazing off some of my hair. A slow ding radiated, like a coin dropping into an empty coin jar. Her knees hit the ground with a thud. Then she fell face down, a gaping hole torn into the rear-middle of the clean curly hair that faced me moments earlier. Bloodstains dotted her sparkling shirt collar. She lay on the ground—lifeless.

I raised a hand to my mouth, hyperventilating, screaming inside but hearing no sound. My eyes burned with shock and threatened to pop out of their sockets. How? *What* happened? One minute there was calm, the next moment chaos in stillness.

I spun toward the direction the bullet came from. Sunlight glinted off another glass-walled high-rise. The glare obscured not only the probable shooter but also the shape of the windows. I swung around again to the scene before me, my breath raggedly out of rhythm. I placed one hand on my heart to keep me from fainting. Then I lowered to a squat to catch my breath.

My gaze fell irresistibly to the slender body slumped down just a few feet from me. Reality drove through me like a nail through wood. My fingers trembled, and my knees threatened to buckle. I was gasping for precious oxygen—which felt suddenly scarce. My eyes traveled the length and breadth of my surroundings. Sounds of my crunchy footsteps on gravel assured me there was no one else left here but me. The construction crew I had heard earlier had gone completely still. I glanced upward. Surely, the shooter didn't see her give me the item earlier or I'd be dead too.

I wrapped my arms tight around myself while visually scouring the spot where I thought I'd heard a ding. The space she directly faced was missing its glass before the shot came through, so there was no broken glass. *Ha! How convenient.* This could make a forensic determination of her murder next to impossible, I thought. Any shred of evidence would be deemed circumstantial—unless there was an eyewitness cum suspect.

I swallowed hard. There was no way this looked good for me. Convincing anyone of what I just saw would be like trying to explain how a tornado could reduce an entire town to rubble but leave one house standing a couple of meters away from the path of destruction. That would be a tough sell, though true.

To my dismay, now I knew why they sent me here. To be the fall girl for a murder I didn't commit. My mind raced through several options, and none of them were appealing. My head swam. I staggered, struggling to stand straight. I made to lean on part of the high-rise structure for support but thought twice about it. The last thing I needed was for my fingerprints to be on anything here.

I began walking away clutching my purse, and I

didn't look back. I pressed my trembling lips closed while my knees were still wobbling. I couldn't swallow the fact that an innocent woman just got murdered right in front of me. I would not—and could not—let it go. I had to do something. And I knew exactly what.

2

...THERE IS A FRIEND WHO STICKS CLOSER THAN A BROTHER.

-Proverbs 18:24

"**R**ed? Are you all right?" Robert asked as I unlocked my door, with his six-foot frame filling the doorway nicely.

"Yeah, I'm fine." I showed him into my apartment. "Red, you're always good at breaking stuff. The way you sounded—I wondered, what did you break this time to get your voice all shaky?" His lips curved upward in a mischievous smile. His eyes fiercely bore into mine, searching for clues, but I gave nothing away. He averted his gaze and studied the apartment. Full eyelashes helped obscure the ill-timed humor beginning to light his eyes, but the squint on his forehead gave him away. Other times I would laugh, but this time I exhaled.

He called me Red instead of Ruby most times. I liked the nickname, so I didn't protest. I swallowed hard and began walking toward the bathroom. Robert followed me.

"It's the bathroom water pipe," I explained in an even tone. "I think I broke it when I came home and decided to take a shower." We both entered the bathroom, and I shut the door.

"Wait, you took two showers in one morning? Must be one errand too many that you ran," he quipped, some hesitancy lacing his voice.

I looked up. *Good.* My plan was working. Vapor filled the room. *Just a few more seconds...*

"Well, you know how old this building is. Given a choice, would I live in a place this aged?" I asked, knowing his answer whether he said it or not.

He shook his head, and a muscle twitched along his sharp jawline, more out of habit. "You'll never leave your precious elderly clients even if you got a million dollars. Admit it." He pouted as the eyeglasses sitting atop his straight nose took on more vapor and began slipping.

At that point, the fog almost fully obscured his face on the bathroom mirror. *Perfect.* I walked over to the showerhead where water still gushed. "Here, please give me a hand."

He didn't move. I turned around, and bent over the water pipe to look toward him. His face had turned beet red.

"Red." Alarm darkened his green eyes. "Please step away from there. That's very hot water." He reached out as though he wanted to pluck me up and out in one fell swoop.

I laughed, although the heat was truly starting to get to me, but I hid it. Now wasn't the time to shy from pain. Something more important was at stake. "Hey. You know we're not six anymore. Stop treating me like a little girl you need to protect. Now, come over here and help me, will you?" If he didn't come close enough to me soon, I may lose the opportunity forever. I beckoned him with a quick wave.

He stepped closer, took off his glasses, and pocketed them, slipping on contacts instead. "The glasses are customized, so I can't afford to ruin them," he added. He was still a bit far but now close enough.

"Robert, listen carefully. I have been framed for murder. I went to a delivery pickup site. The requester paid me well—ten thousand bucks." So I related what happened. "Before they shot her, she said something about a surveillance thing called The New Rulebook. She said they see everything. She then handed me a journal. I read the first few pages on my way home. She wrote that thick water vapor can cloud their monitoring ability, but only for a short period."

His eyes widened as I narrated, lips pressing firmly as his naturally-shaped, perfect brows arched in unison when I stopped speaking—the way they always did when he was in deep thought. He ran a quick hand through his hair while the other hand settled on his waist. He closed the small gap between us, stopping inches from me. "That's why you broke the pipe."

"Exactly. I had no choice."

He bent over slightly, arching over the gushing water, then forcefully stopped its flow with a hand plug. Almost immediately, the vapor began to clear as Robert and I finished reattaching the pipe onto the showerhead. I spoke faster, providing him with every detail of the occurrence.

Robert had known me all my life, and right now, I needed someone who required very few words to understand me. It didn't hurt to have that someone also be a policeman.

H alf an hour later, I was still clad in the outfit I wore on assignment this morning. I shifted and tugged at my shirt, smoothing away creases. Even though my hands were busy, I had been listening to the news through my embedded earpieces. News of her murder hadn't broken in the media yet, though I wished I could glue myself down in front of the TV right now to see when it did.

Although I was preoccupied, I made a mental note to thank Robert for these earpieces later. They were his gift to me last Christmas. Then I didn't understand why he was so into tech breakthroughs, but now, I was sure glad he was. The earpieces were structured to transmit audio from any active technological gadget, whether radio, TV, or PC from everywhere across my apartment, whether they were configured or not. In contrast, Robert's job seemed worlds apart from his passion for technology, but he fit into both worlds naturally at the same time. He was always saying "you can't fight crime without tech" whenever I raised the topic.

"We need to get out of here right away," he shouted from the bathroom, snapping me back to the moment. Seconds later, he approached while wiping his wet hands with a towel. A rough trail of dampened toilet paper stuck to the sole of his shoe followed behind.

So I stepped on the tip as he passed by, breaking it off.

He turned around, picked it up, and then rolled it into a ball. "Thanks. The tub's all fixed up now."

He paused, pressing his lips together and lowering his voice. "Red, you should never have come back here after the lady was killed. We leave now, and you never return—*ever*. Do you understand?"

Shaken, I nodded, unable to manage anything more. I headed to my bedroom and started packing a few belongings.

Robert moved around the house peering into every corner with a flashlight, lifting some old phone books on a bookcase and attracting a sneeze. I figured he was probably searching for signs of surveillance equipment. I doubted they'd put it where someone could easily find it.

I smiled sadly. Usually, sleep was the only thing I craved when my day was over. Until today. Until now, when all I wanted was safety—and answers—while fleeing my only home. Exasperated, I sighed as I finally tucked my last item—a framed photo of me as a little girl—into a duffel bag.

Robert came up behind me and patted my shoulder. He then bent over and pulled my daily journal containing my business contacts out of the bag, tossing it back onto the bed. "Red, I'm sorry, but you can't use those anymore. You're saying goodbye to your life as you know it. I understand this is new territory for you, but you're going to have to trust me." Sudden wrinkles lined his forehead.

Tears were brimming to the surface, but I fought them down. I sat on the bed and brought my knees up to my jaw, throwing my head backward for a moment. Pouring my hair together onto my right shoulder, I twisted the tip of a strand, absentmindedly wishing none of this were happening to me.

With concern lining his brow, he squatted and took my hand. "I'm going to get you to safety first then find out who's behind this, how big this thing is, okay? I might be doing this in reverse, but I'm not going to call this in to the station just yet. If I do, it could spook them." He gave me a look tough to decipher. "There's something I've got to tell you now in case I can't tell you later."

But I barely heard him above my worried heart. I tore my eyes away and gazed out the window. I wished that those behind this setup would tell me why me. That's what I wanted—no, *needed*—to know right now. Rising, I walked toward the clear, crisp view. My feet knocked down my journal partway there, which was perched slightly off the bed. It slid all the way onto the floor, stopping near the wall crest of the window. I got closer to pick it up. "Robert, I—"

A piercing sound whizzed into my earpieces and broke my stride. "My ear!" I bent over and yanked off each earpiece, tossing them. When I straightened, Robert was facing the window, his eyes fixed on a point past me. With my breathing ragged, I looked behind me. Shards of glass poured onto my back like confetti.

"Get down!" Robert yelled.

I complied.

He yanked his radio from his belt. But a second wave of shattering panes followed from the adjacent window. I dove beneath my study desk, kicking the chair out to fit me in under. I felt the searing pain of a sharp cut, but I was too high strung to know exactly where.

"Red! Look!"

I shrank back as two crossed ropes I didn't previously see knotted powerfully right where I would have stood. One leg of my tossed chair spun into the knot of the ropes. The empty seat now facing out dragged forward then lodged on the windowsill, tipping almost over the ledge. My mouth slid agape in shock. "Unbelievable." My hands wound like a vise onto the sides of my study desk.

"Oh, Jesus!" Robert mumbled in prayer while panting. I didn't know when he became religious. And I didn't seriously care right now. Silence gradually returned, interrupted by leftover particles dropping onto the ground.

When I could hear above the drumming beat of my own heart, I turned toward him. "Robert?"

He pointed across the floor from where I lay. "Suicide." Our eyes met. "It would've looked like you committed—"

I nodded. "I know. Like I jumped off the window to hang myself." I planted my palms on the ground, using my big toe to drag down my duffel bag. Blood dripped behind my ankle where, apparently, I'd gotten a cut.

"Red. Head to the living room. I'll grab the bag."

I took his hand. He drew me by the armpits toward himself. We lay inches from each other.

"They'll think you're dead." He rolled over and leaned up on his elbow, a wry smile crossing his chiseled face. "Let's make 'em think they're right." His gritte-toothed response mirrored my determination to survive. He handed over his radio.

I crawled through the bedroom door to the living room on hands and knees, while Robert trailed close behind.

~

We both crawled into the living room. The blinds were still closed from when I'd shut them earlier. We rose as we neared the couch.

"They must've used a proximity alert to trigger pressure on the window panes causing them to blow. There could be more of 'em. We need to move now." Robert dusted himself off while he rose to his feet.

But I didn't budge. "Why me? Why are they doing this to me?"

He came close, squatted, and peered into my face, taking my arm with one hand, the other held up for caution. He treated me as though I was as fragile as the just-broken glass.

"I know you didn't kill anyone, okay?" His eyes grew gentle as they scanned my face.

I said nothing. Instead, I raised a finger in an attempt to calm my trembling lips.

"But I'm still a police officer. And I follow the law."

"So, are you going to turn me in right away?"

He shook his head, waving a defensive hand in the air. "That's not what I'm saying. As you are an eyewitness to murder and a possible person of interest, the law needs to know your whereabouts. You just need to keep calm and cooperate. Meanwhile, I'll ask at the station about The New Rulebook." His eyebrows arched upward in thought. "The name sounds familiar for some reason. For now, we need to move."

He let go of my hand and grabbed my duffel bag. I rose with new resolve and shook my head vigorously, arms akimbo. "No, Robert. I'm not running away. I don't have a reason to."

I turned, but he grabbed my arm. I snapped it back from him in defiance. "Listen to me." My voice sounded like it was breaking, but I couldn't care less. "I've worked too hard and too long for some folks just to show up out of nowhere and take everything away in a flash." I held in a sob, trying hard to keep it down. "I'm not going to leave my house or my life for anyone. Someone or something will prove my innocence."

Robert moved in closer, close enough I could smell his cologne. "And by then you could be long dead. You have to trust me. There is no other way." He interlocked his left fingers to mine—our symbol of unity of purpose when we were younger.

I was trembling all over now as the truth of his words found acknowledgment in my heart. I knew he was right. Though, unfortunately so. I also knew I was way over my head. Tough business clients I could handle, but smart psychopaths were beyond my skill set.

Words were no longer necessary. He pulled me into an embrace while sobs wracked my body. I freed the tears that had been brimming inside me since this ordeal started and clung to his strong arms like I was literally holding on for dear life. His hands stroked my back, though giving little comfort inside. Moments later, my sobs quieted. We separated, and I took some tissue to wipe my face. Perching on the couch, I cupped my face in both hands.

Robert inhaled deeply and observed me with concern lining his brow. He sat next to me and offered a tentative smile, his green eyes sharing my pain. "Red, I promise you, I will get you somewhere safe and keep it known only to me until someone else becomes need-to-know. You are the toughest person I know, and you will get through this." He squeezed my arm. "Here, take this." He handed me the apartment key. "You never know."

I looked at it and smiled a little.

He walked back to the bathroom and returned with a first-aid kit. "We need to tend to that foot."

Oh, I had forgotten about the injury, focusing instead on having survived a suicide frame-up.

He lifted my foot and wiped the blood off several times with an alcohol prep pad. It tingled, and I sucked in my breath.

"There. All better." He covered it with a Band-Aid and patted it lightly.

I nodded. "Thanks."

Just then, something blared on the TV like breaking news. He stepped away to replace the kit while I got on my feet and moved forward to listen.

Then all I could do was point to the TV. My feet stuck to the floor as though with glue. Her face was splashed across the 37-inch screen. Breath whistled past my teeth as I blinked hard. She stared at me, like a ghost from the distant past. Only it was this morning. "Robert! Look."

He returned and glanced up at the screen. "They found her."

I nodded, unable to speak anymore. "How?" I croaked out.

Then Robert moved like lightning, dashing across the living room, unplugging electronic gadgets, knocking out lightbulbs on the chandelier with his arm protected by a cloth-glove. He looked at me with half-crazed eyes, wiping his face in between heaved breaths. "If they planted something here to see you with, it most definitely needs a power source, and if not, then it's probably attached to a light fixture. I'm just guessing, but I might be right."

I was still stuck in the same spot, mouth agape, eyes wide. My mind whirled wildly like a wind gauge, trying to fit all the pieces together.

"Forget the TV. The police—and the people who framed you—will be here soon. They may even be watching and listening to us. We have to go now."

Deep inside, I was still hoping for another way out of this situation. "The police, at least, have no way of tying me to this. I mean, for all the world knows, I wasn't anywhere near there today. I can give back their money too."

He shook his head and tapped his foot repeatedly on the ground.

I didn't care if he was impatient. I was only going to run if all else failed.

"You said earlier that your hair was grazed off at the crime scene, right?" He pointed to the screen. "You're almost the same height as the woman on TV. You can be certain that the police will check public and police surveillance cameras soon. Once they place you at or near the crime scene, you'll be a suspect—probably the *sole* suspect." A troubled frown followed. "With those people who set you up, we could have mere minutes, and with the police, maybe a couple of days to process your hair sample and get results from the lab."

He scratched his head, causing some of his glossy

brown hair to tumble onto his hand. "I'm sad even to think this, but if these people have moles within the police, we may have less time than I predicted."

My mouth dropped open, and my world shattered like a wrecking ball would rip apart a house. "But—" I protested, searching for a reason to say why this was all wrong.

"Don't you get it?" He grabbed my shoulders. "They sent you there because they needed someone to take the fall. That makes you their fall guy. You fit their perfect frame-up all around. You can be sure they planted enough motive to pin this on you. I'm very sorry, Red."

Premature wrinkle lines formed on his forehead while his voice deepened further. "It's better for you to assume that you could be a murder suspect right now than otherwise. Assuming they heard everything we just said, from however the murdered lady claims they see and hear, time's probably up." He grabbed my elbow. "C'mon." He picked up the duffel bag.

I tried to walk, but my feet did not budge.

"Now! Ruby," he insisted, pulling me along.

But I was in shock. My predicament was dawning on me all at once. Within moments, I began to function again. We ran out of my apartment, and for the first time, I did not lock it. I took one more look and swallowed hard as the only safe haven I had known since the orphanage disappeared behind me, while I ran toward an uncertain future.

We hurried down a couple flights of stairs side by

side, turning toward the exit. We reached the ground floor, making for the main building's door.

A muscular man seeming about six feet tall, slammed right into us at the doorway, panting. His gaze darted between Robert and me. His eyes then settled on me without doubt.

I peered down at his hands—he held a gun in one and a satellite radio in the other. A gasp escaped my throat. My feet suddenly grew wobbly, like jelly. A muffled shot rang out just as my world went black.

3

DO NOT BE AFRAID... ONLY BELIEVE. -MARK 5:36

"You might want to keep your head down, Red." Head cushioned on a pillow, I turned my neck sideways toward the familiar deep voice.

Emerald-green eyes gazed into mine, sparkling though edged with worry. He smiled. His gaze sharp as an eagle's looked me over with careful scrutiny.

I used my elbow to push up to a half-leaning position. "What's going on?" Sharp pain throbbed through my head like a relentless hammer, answering my question. "Uh." I sighed, reluctantly lying back down. The memory of what happened poured in unbidden. I gasped and looked up at Robert. "How did we—" With one hand, I rubbed away to soothe my aching forehead.

A grin spread across his face. Then he rose to full height. "Get away?"

He strode to a granite-layered counter and returned with a glass of water. He leaned over then lowered the glass to my lips. With one firm arm cupping the back of my head, he prodded me. "Drink up. You need it."

I hesitated because I've never liked drinking water. He knew that. But gulping down twice, I avoided a lecture. Last time he did this, we were thirteen. I'd climbed a tree in the orphanage's school playground then took a fall from the branch. I ended up with cuts, bruises—and high fever within hours. Robert had lectured me for up to two hours before I accepted the nurse's aspirin.

"Want an aspirin?"

I shook my head, eyelids growing heavy. I caught a knowing smile forming at the corners of his mouth.

"Didn't think so," he muttered, setting the glass on a center table located an arm's length away.

I looked around, sensing familiarity. "Where is this, Robert?"

He perched near my feet, seated at the edge of the tan leopard-print couch where I lay. He held up a hand. "I'll take it one question at a time, princess. Okay, now the answer to your first, you fell."

"What do you mean, 'I fell'?" I sensed a frown creasing my forehead. I spread out the couch throw already over me around my middle section more comfortably.

"It all happened really fast. You passed out when

the guy held up a gun to shoot you. That threw him off. Can't shoot someone if they're already down, right? So I caught you with one hand, and then kicked the gun out his hand with my right foot, just as the shot went off. Luckily, we weren't hit. Next, I pulled my weapon on him, stopping him."

I inched the pillow a bit higher. "If you caught me, why is my head throbbing hard as an old locomotive train?"

He ran a hand through his hair, lips thinning at the same time. "I *may*—and I insist, may—have accidentally bumped your head against my knee when I kicked him." His shoulders inched upward defensively while his arms flew outward.

"You did what?!"

He quickly continued, more in an attempt to stop the coming tirade. "It was a mistake. Truly. I'm sorry about that. And the answer to your second question, we're still in your building, two floors below yours. At the apartment on the ground floor." He cleared his throat and cast a furtive glance.

My face could still be showing how angry I was because his voice became a little high-pitched like whenever he'd really gotten on my wrong side. Police sirens passively rang in from the street through cracks in the parted window shutters, cutting into our conversation. Then they faded. But I said nothing while lost in thought.

He moved closer and cradled my hand. "I'm truly sorry if my knee is what hurt you, okay? You know I'd never intentionally do so. My reaction was impromptu. I just—I had to do do *something*."

I nodded slightly, feeling relieved. "It's all right. I'll get better." I adjusted to lie on my side.

"That was quick, Red. You sure? Or you'll get your pound of flesh later?" As I flipped back around, he tipped the side of his face to me, his Adam's apple bobbing as he spoke. "Do it if it makes you feel any better."

At first, I didn't get it. Then when realization dawned, I rose sharply, ignoring my swaying neck, now lacking its supportive pillow. "You know what, now I'm *really* offended that you would even suggest that!" I was panting now, unsure whether it was due to anger or the stubborn ache zapping through my head and worsening by the minute. He raised a hand in objection, but I shrugged him off. "I may be in pain, but I'm not stupid."

"I—" he interjected.

Now, I held up a warning hand. "No, Robert. I don't want to hear it. You tell me what happened—everything—and exactly the way it happened. That's all I want to hear from you right now."

His shoulders heaved, a deep breath escaped his lips, and sculpted biceps moved in unison. "When you passed out, I secured the guy's gun. He tried to call someone on the SAT phone, but I aimed my weapon at him, forcing him to stop. You were still out so I couldn't move us from here without having to carry you all the way—and that would've certainly raised eyebrows on the street. So, I cuffed him to the stairwell and called it in to the station as an armed intruder situation. Apparently, he was sent in here alone. I threatened to shoot him if he moved a step. He dropped his phone to the ground. I stomped it, breaking off the antenna."

"And where was I?"

He pointed out toward the door. "Behind the stairwell. You were passed out for three and half hours. I'm not proud to say this, but I'd hoped you'd stay out till the police were done and gone. And you did." He sighed then leaned back against the couch. "When they left, an elderly lady came out of this apartment and asked me to bring you inside. She'd witnessed everything through her peephole. She said you were a good girl and thanked me for not handing you over to the cops." He chuckled.

"Yeah, she didn't know you were one of 'em. What happened to your uniform?" I asked, looking him over briefly.

He glanced downward. "I got these from your duffel bag. I bet I look cool in female yoga pants and tees, huh? Errr! Not a word, Ruby. I need to change back into uniform as soon as my clothes are out of her dryer."

I laughed heartily—observing the snugly-fitted pink shirt worn over now high-cropped black workout pants—until an ache in my temple interrupted me. "I most likely know our host. Where is she right now?" I searched the apartment for the lady in question.

He pointed to the door. "She said she'd take a long

walk several times around the block to make sure you were safe."

"Are you serious?" I chuckled, quite perplexed. "Why would you let an elderly woman hike around the block as security? You might give her arthritis by the day's end if not get her killed, Robert."

His eyebrows arched in unison. Mouth agape, he shrank back, shaking his head vigorously. "Wait, I didn't ask her to do *anything*. I tried to stop her, but she wouldn't listen. She said she was your very first delivery client, and without you, she'd have to fight through human bowling pins—her words, not mine —to get groceries at the store. It seems you're well valued around here."

I sat up now, totally ignoring the pain. "Ms. Paula Bryant. Oh no! Robert, we have to leave. She's such a nice lady. I don't want her to be in harm's way because of this mess. We need to leave—now." I peeled back the throws that had enveloped me with warmth and looked around the floor for my shoes, bracing my head with one hand.

Robert was still sitting. I scowled at him. "What are you waiting for? We can't stay here. Get your clothes from the dryer." He scratched his clean-shaven beard line, but I resisted rolling my eyes. "C'mon, Emerald Eyes, let's go."

That got him on his feet—and smiling. "Okay, *Madame* Red. I'll grab 'em."

～

"One more minute...I don't want to catch a cold in these," Robert shouted from the laundry room adjacent to Ms. Bryant's kitchen a half hour later.

"Okay." I snapped the rear of my comfort shoes snug. "I'm in the living room." I tapped on the ground, testing the shoes' fit on my injured foot. I heard a rap and cast a glance at the door then twisted toward the kitchen. Robert must still be drying his clothes.

The knock sounded again, faster this time, and a tad impatient. Ms. Bryant had probably returned from her walk. I rose and walked to the door to get it. Closing one eye, I looked through the peephole. Before I could make anything out, hands grabbed my waist from behind. A firm hand muzzled my attempt to scream. My heart rate rose as I was hustled backward through the apartment, to the kitchen.

"It's me," Robert whispered into my ear. He set me on my feet in the middle of the kitchen, then reached out one hand to the adjacent wall and turned off the lights. "The kitchen doors have an extra lock with keys. The keys aren't there, so we can't get out that way. But I discovered a large pet exit at the bottom of the kitchen's back door. We could squeeze through. Come on." He barely lifted his voice above a whisper. He led to the exit, but when I grabbed his arm and sprung him back, he turned around.

"Wait, where's Ms. Bryant?" What if she's in harm's way already?

Light air blew on my cheek as he exhaled deeply.

"I'm sorry, Red, but I don't know. The one thing I know for sure is that it's not her rapping at her own front door. She took her keys with her when she left."

Crack. Wood ripped in the front room as someone broke down the door, forcing it off its hinges. *Definitely couldn't be Ms. Bryant doing it.* "So how do I know she's okay, Robert? How?"

"Right now, there's no way for us to be sure." He took both of my hands and guided them toward the bottom of the door until I felt the wooden frame. "But wherever she is, she would want you to remain safe, and I'm going to make sure you are. Let's go. You first."

Following his guidance, I bent down on hands and knees and reached for the flap lid over the pet exit. But I still couldn't help wondering. Why did my world keep unraveling deeper and faster every time I opened my eyes? The raspy voices grew closer. Raising the thick plastic flap, I squeezed both arms in one after the other, while sucking in my breath so my midsection could easily glide through. I shifted sideways as my hips briefly wedged stuck.

"Hurry!" Robert pushed my feet, helping unhinge my hips.

I scrambled out onto my feet as he forced the duffel bag out next. So I grabbed it. His head appeared. Then he slid the rest of him underneath more easily, using the edges to push free.

We raced across the small yard. Angry voices rose in unison within the apartment. Then the kitchen lights came back on. Behind the curtain, I spotted the shadows of people bending over, searching around, and slamming dish cupboards as though we were small enough to fit into them. I tore my eyes away and faced forward. Sprinting down the street, we paused near a sharp curve where a combined garbage collection bin stood tall. "Officer, do you need assistance? I can help call someone. I've got a cell phone," a young, average-height, brown-skinned man asked Robert.

But...how'd he know Robert was an officer? I glanced at Robert. Then I saw he was back in uniform. The pink tee underneath still glared abstractly out of his one-buttoned down shirt. I hadn't seen his wardrobe change as I'd barely glanced when we made it out of Ms. Bryant's. So his outfit had been a blur.

Robert reached out and accepted the cell phone with a nod. "Thank you, sir." He cast a cautious glance behind us, dialed quickly, and then brought the phone to his ear.

"Hey, man. I've got a problem. I need you out here on Sandy Drive. You remember where Ruby lives, right?" He paused for a response on the other end then nodded. "Yes, we'll be two blocks from here at a coffee shop, at the right corner. And please keep this between me and you, partner. See you soon." He handed the phone back to the stranger. "Thank you so much, sir. We appreciate your help."

The man smiled and nodded. "Glad to help out, officer. Good luck." He rejoined pedestrian traffic headed downtown while we made our way on foot in the opposite direction, toward The Unique specialty coffee and teashop.

We stopped briefly while I grabbed a yellow-flowered spring scarf from the duffel bag to use it for a partial disguise, knotting it around my neck as we hurried along. For all anyone could tell, he was an officer on duty. During the pause, he did, however, fully button up his shirt.

"Robert." I drew in a deep breath, carefully choosing my words. "Just in case I don't make it out of this alive, I—"

He walked back in two wide strides, stopping me in my tracks. He waved a hand in the air, eyes wide and furious. "Okay, now you've gone too far. In this situation, we don't talk like that—at all. It's got to be your bad head making you say stuff. Here's an icepack." He directed the icepack to my forehead like stray gear, placing my hand over it, as though that was the panacea to my statement. Yet he still firmly took and held my free hand as we walked along. I yielded, dropping the matter.

Not long afterward, we reached the end of the street. The Unique, just across from where we were, bustled with eager customers lined up for their daily taste fest, which happened for an hour every evening. The scent of rare coffee and flavored herbal tea welcomed us to the shop. We crossed at the traffic light and joined other patrons who chatted happily, oblivious to our plight.

Robert stood tall, busy looking around and scanning the crowd for any threats. His gaze met mine, eyes brimming with raw determination. "Red, I need you to listen to what I'm about to say." He pulled me closer, briefly separating us from the others in line.

Some customers sent friendly glances our way. I smiled back in return, but Robert was too preoccupied to notice their kind gesture.

Music danced into my ears from within the store. So I let myself savor the moment, loosening my hair from its bun and letting it glide free. I danced in full surrender, losing the stress of the whole day with each swirl. If my life was at risk, then I'd cherish every moment of happiness from now on—including this one. I slowed to a stop, recalling where we were. I must have closed my eyes because when I opened them, others were dancing along while waiting in line, moving steadily toward the door. Robert stared at me from a distance with a look I couldn't explain. "You okay?" I asked, a little worried.

He took my hand, cradling it in his. I might've seen moisture in his eyes, but he quickly blinked it away. He closed his eyes for a moment and drew in a deep breath. When he opened them, they were mistier. "Red. I promise you, I will not let anything happen to you." He nodded, as though to let his words sink in, more for him than for me. "If this gets more out of hand than it already is, and I'm just saying *if*, then I'll officially place you into protective custody and personally escort you to the station. Please don't scare me again with such speculations like you did earlier. Please, Red?"

I nodded. "All right then." We got back in line just

as we neared the double-door entrance. I looked up at him. "If you do bring me in, what are you going to tell your boss to make him know I'm innocent and not a murderer?"

He leaned on a railing by the doorway. "Psshh... Right now, I don't know. But when the time comes, I'll think of something."

I chuckled while accepting our sample cups of tea and coffee. "Another lie? Robert Towers, you've—"

"Never lied to you." He whipped around. "What's the first lie?" His jaw tightened, and his face looked like he was between anger and dreadful anticipation of my response.

"Promising me that I'll be okay."

As we entered the shop, I scouted out some seats near the door. Just then, Robert faced me, a fiercely protective look in his eyes I hadn't seen this clearly before. "I didn't lie about that. I'll do everything in my power, though I'm well aware of my human limits. You have to believe you'll make it through this, or else... You can't give up just yet, Red."

I stepped closer, shaking my head. "Who's talking about giving up? Of course, I'm not giving up. I'm just saying that I'm not going to put you in harm's way in order to stay safe. Your life is equally valuable to me. That's all I'm saying, and I mean it."

He ground his teeth but kept his thoughts to himself. But I wouldn't complain. After all, that about suited my mood right now.

We pulled our chairs back and sat down. I settled our tea and coffee on the table. His face was void of expression like he was in some faraway land. Occasionally, I had no way of knowing what was going on behind those green eyes. I watched the reflections change while he sipped tea to help drive his thoughts home, while I drank coffee for a while.

When he looked up, he seemed calmer so that calmed me too. "Sorry for my tone earlier. Maybe I was being overprotective."

I smiled weakly. "I understand. We need to be hopeful but also practical. We have to accept that things could go wrong. Not that it's what I hope happens but..." I trailed off, not ready to consider everything that could go wrong which hadn't already.

"You are going to be okay, Red. I promise—again. 'Bout what you inferred earlier, I enforce and obey the law. I don't lie to the law—*ever*. And I *did not* lie when I said you'd be all right—because you will." He smiled with practiced formality. So I knew someone else was about to join our table.

"Hey, buddy," the voice came from behind me, "are you okay? My car's outside. Let's go if you're ready." It sounded like Jim Phillips, Robert's partner. We both stood up, leaving our half-empty cups behind. Skipping pleasantries, we walked behind Jim toward the exit.

4

─────────

WITH THE LORD, ONE DAY IS LIKE A THOUSAND YEARS, AND
a thousand years like one day. -2Peter 3:8

"Tell me, again, everything you remember
about the shot. From the moment you
became aware of it." Robert honked at a
rough driver cutting sharply into our lane. He was
typically the most patient driver I'd ever seen—until
today. Matter of fact, I didn't think I'd ever heard him
toot his horn at anyone before—no matter what.

He threw me an I-know-you-saw-that glance, but
all things considered, I said nothing. This was no ordinary day. There was no need to be surprised by
unusual behavior from anyone—especially Robert. In
contrast, Jim remained silent, sitting in the seat
behind me, completely engrossed in his own
thoughts. With his recent divorce just concluded, I

certainly didn't blame him for his refrain. Though I wished I could share his calm.

"It was a clean shot. Well...almost clean. It brushed off some of my hair. I still can't get that picture out of my head. I mean, who does that? Shoots an innocent lady?" I sighed. "Whoever these people are, three things are clear: one, they planned this way ahead of time; two, they planned things to the exact detail; and three, they're very dangerous. We shouldn't be messing with them—except they messed with us first. Come to think of it, what were the odds that I'd walk to the window in my apartment this morning, eh? There's so much we don't know."

We made a turn and drew to a slow stop. Robert properly parked, glancing at his partner in the back seat. "Thanks, buddy, for getting us out of there. We're only going to be gone for a couple of minutes." He handed Jim the car keys and accepted another set of keys—house keys—in exchange.

Jim stepped out of the car, swung around, and glided into the driver's seat. "I'll be waiting here. You both hurry, or we'll get caught in downtown evening rush-hour traffic."

We hurried up a flight of stairs, stopping at an apartment on the left side. Robert unlocked the door and turned the knob, proceeding with cautious steps as we entered. A rustic smell greeted us. Pictures of Jim with his ex-wife and son lined the wall. My heart hurt for them. This must be the house Robert mentioned that Jim had moved out of and was trying to put on the market.

"There should be some feminine items still left in the restroom. Hurry, please. We leave in fifteen minutes."

I carted the duffel bag along with me, intent on safeguarding The New Rulebook journal inside. "Okay. I won't be long." I entered the bathroom and shut the door. Exactly what sanitary action could I achieve in fifteen minutes? But rather than freezing, I'd better make the most of what little time I had here.

I shook my hair loose, and its locks cascaded down to my shoulders free of the bun I'd re-pinned them in during the ride. I gathered my thoughts, interrupted when I caught my reflection in the mirror. I stared at my reflection. How could I wash off the look of shock still plastered on my face? Or fix the dull ache throbbing in my heart within fifteen minutes? Specks of dust from the pet exit out of Ms. Bryant's house appeared still caught in parts of my hair, with some even on my face. Streaks of deep-brown foundation powder smeared under my eyes. Mascara ran partially at the corners of my eyelids. My clothes were creased in the wrong places, and sweat dampened the neck of my shirt, sending a chill over me.

Tears flowed down my face, and sobs came through. I shielded my mouth with my hands pressed tightly on it so Robert wouldn't hear me and grow concerned. Then I closed the toilet seat and sat on it, relieving my buckling knees of their burden. Moments later, I gathered myself together and splashed cold water on my face, scrubbing my skin to wash it out. I saw how the different colors flowing into the sink told the story of how my day went so far.

"We've got to go, Red." Robert rapped on the door. So I jerked in subconscious reaction before I found my voice. "Sure. I'll be right there." I changed into clean clothes, packed the soiled ones into a bag, and secured it with a sling-type rope. I stepped out of the bathroom, feeling physically cleaner and emotionally lighter, while grateful for this much-needed bathroom break.

Robert stood right by the front door, only yards away from me. "Are you ready?"

I nodded and looked away quickly, not trusting my voice. He paused then went ahead without asking. We stepped out, and he shut the apartment door then locked it. We reached the car and climbed in with Jim now in the driver's seat.

Robert handed over the house keys. "Thanks, man. We'll catch a taxi from here."

Jim nodded. "Anytime, buddy. I'm on leave starting tomorrow for two weeks. I'm going to see family in Rhode Island. Call me if you need anything. You both be careful now."

I forcefully tore my eyes off Robert's ill-fitted shirt and color-riot wear. This was very different from his usual well-tailored, stylish look. I sighed and pursed my lips. We were now living like fugitives—all because of me. And that had to change.

∼

"You should be safe here." Robert passed me bottled water. When I'd asked him to stop so we could buy some drinking water on our way here, he'd insisted that we needed to stay off locations with cameras. He made sense, so I endured the thirst— for two long hours. Since I rarely drank water, there was no way he could have envisaged this turn of events.

I felt my eyes narrow when I glanced toward him. "What do you mean 'you'? I thought we're both on the run here. Are you quitting on me already?" I tugged at the hem of his shirt playfully.

His shoulders shook with laughter. "You haven't lost your sense of humor, huh?" He received the duffel bag from me. "You're still not out of danger yet. I need to make a few calls so I can't stay just yet. The people after you—let's hope they're still in the dark about how you got out of the building."

Something about his tone set me on edge. I couldn't put a finger on it, though, so I let it go. If it was important, he'd tell me at the right time.

"What's this place, Robert?" I examined the apartment more closely, my eyes adjusting to the dim indoor lighting. An empty, gold-painted art frame stood at the right corner of the living room, obscuring part of the sole window's view. No fancy decorations were there, just one oak center table, one white couch with two gold-embroidered, checkered throws and two steel side chairs. A desk lamp rested on the edge of the oak table. A false white orchid occupied the center, next to a mini desk clock. Simple, yet very different from the redbrick homes with carefully manicured lawns and estate-like sculptures we'd passed up the street. I didn't mind the simplicity. I was just worried that its contrasting structure amidst a wealthy enclave didn't readily fit in.

I scanned the kitchen area toward the left. An artistic archway led inside. Ceramic dishes sat covered with a protective veil on the counter. One cooking pot stared back at me, glistening like it had never been used. "Only one cooking pot," I muttered. From where I stood, the kitchen looked like it was made more for display than for use, with no sign of wear.

I returned my attention to Robert, who was still standing at the door, watching me closely while I moved deeper into the living room. I wasn't so worried about him since I knew that sometimes he retracted into his shell when he felt overwhelmed like he must have been feeling now. This predicament was eating away at him just like me.

So I asked him a question. "How far?" When he approached, hands in his pockets, I crossed my arms and continued, "Can I get from their reach? Think about it. They paid me ten thousand dollars today for a delivery they knew wouldn't happen."

We simultaneously sat on both steel chairs, facing each other. Though he remained silent.

"The only way they could've safely and comfortably positioned a sniper in a highbrow area, with enough time to escape afterward, was if they had access to or owned an entire floor. Leasing the entire floor of a high-rise building in a prime location with good window view costs at least six figures anywhere in the world."

His face took on a glum look.

I inhaled a deep breath at the repercussions, but I was insistent on getting my next point across, however unpleasant it felt. "Robert, please just take me in. You're a cop. Cuff me and escort me downtown. You can tell them you saw me so you arrested me. Period. That should suffice."

He stared at my extended hands, promptly rising and walking to the window, hands shoved into his pockets again. He then pulled his hands out of pocket and folded them. "These people are millionaires. That's what it means, Red. That's smart. And you're correct." Clearly, he ignored my offer to be arrested by him.

I sighed, rising as well. Then I leaned against the kitchen partition. "This is Chevvy Chase if I read the street signs correctly. Millionaires live in Chevvy Chase. Robert, this is their playground. This is the last place I should be. Maybe the other side of town is best."

"No, that's not a good idea." A muscle tensed along his jawline, and he headed toward the door without explaining his thought.

I stood in his way, now suspecting he was hiding something. He'd never been good at it, at least not with me. I looked him eye to eye with my arms akimbo. "Why, Robert?"

He stopped but still looked away.

"I may not be in law enforcement, but I'm not ignorant. Talk." Insistent, I beckoned him back indoors.

He sighed, and his shoulders dropped as he walked deeper into the apartment, and then sat down. "The poor neighborhood is the wrong place for us to go. That's where they'd look first." He ran a hand through his hair, head thrown backward.

"You're an innocent victim, an amateur at best, so they'll assume that would be your kneejerk reaction. There in the poor neighborhoods, they've got access to traffic cameras all over, but here, I saw less than four traffic and speed cameras on our way, mostly on bridges and school zones. No speed bumps at all. With The New Rulebook, cameras mean eyes in the sky. Here, you hide in plain sight." He raised his head. "For the sake of your peace of mind, I'm staying for a bit, so we can think this through."

But I was only partly relieved. Why did I still feel as though he hadn't told me everything? "Is there something else you haven't told me, Robert?"

He averted his gaze in response. "Red, we're fine."

The blush spreading across his neck said otherwise. Maybe I'd embarrassed him. This day was tough enough already, so I didn't push it.

I stepped out of his way. "If you say so. You should've explained all this earlier so I didn't have to ask."

"Sorry, I've got a lot on my mind."

I nodded, smiling a little. "Yeah, I kind of noticed."

I waited for him to fill in the gaps, but he didn't

explain further. He then smiled too, seeming a bit more relaxed than when we walked in. My heart stirred when I saw the same set of facial features of the six-year-old boy who befriended me eighteen years ago. Green and kind—though sharp—eyes. A set jaw, which was always clean-shaven. Ears easily aligned. A small scar below his upper left jaw, and a dark-spotted birthmark, walnut-sized, pinched his left earlobe. His short brown hair he typically wore trimmed military style, though it was a bit longer now. Yeah, he looked exactly the same, just grown up and stressed out. I sighed, subconsciously heaving my shoulders. "I'm sorry I got you into all this mess."

He shook his head and rose to his feet. "You don't have to apologize for anything. To tell you the truth, I would've been mad if I wasn't your first phone call."

"Though I wish I called for a good reason." I chuckled. "Wait, as a cop, aren't you supposed to tell me to call my lawyer first before talking to you? You know, being a suspect and all..."

He swiveled, and his eyes shone as his lips widened into a smile. "Yeah, Red. Such an amazing pseudocriminal you are. If all criminals are like you, I would've caught 'em all, and maybe become chief of police or mayor by now."

I shrugged. "Hey, I'm trying real hard here. Give me some credit."

He grinned, giving me a quick side hug, and then faced me fully, cupping both my shoulders. "You're the last person this should happen to—and I'm not just saying so because I know you." His eyes softened, roamed all over my face, and then he glanced away quickly—again.

A catch in his voice raised my internal red flags, but I tamped them down and cautioned myself. For all it was worth, I was probably overreacting to everything given recent events. Maybe I just needed some sleep. I glanced around, searching. "Where's the bathroom?"

He pointed to the inner unlit corner. "The light switch's on the left side wall." He grabbed the duffel bag, coming up behind me.

I waved for him to stop. "No, you stay with the bag. I need a hot shower. Then we're going to brainstorm our way out of this."

Nodding, he headed back toward the living room. "Sounds like a plan."

∼

"Y ou should rest."

Sheets of paper ruffled as I rose to grab my umpteenth cup of coffee. "Nope. There's no time to rest yet. Every minute counts, you said so yourself. We've got to get ahead of these people."

He moved the bowl of popcorn we'd been snacking endlessly on, from the couch to the oak table.

"Let's rehearse what we know of the murdered lady." I gave my fresh brew to Robert to hold for me. After settling on the couch, I accepted it back from him. "Thanks."

He nodded absentmindedly, eyes still scouring the pages. "Sure."

We'd split the journal into two. He read the hardbound notes, while I read the many clipped sheets, held together by an eagle-wings-shaped binder clip.

"I discovered she's a computer analyst with Cortexe Corp., though I'm pretty sure she did more than just analysis, especially with her creating The New Rulebook. Her name is Violet Zendel, and I got that from page one. These sheets—though loose— were all numbered, and they're full of intricate drawings, maybe of things, places, or events, I'm not sure. I need to dig deeper. I can't do it without a computer." He rubbed his eyes, settling his elbow on his knee, with one hand supporting his jaw. "The journal itself has records mostly documenting her experiences with colleagues and a certain *Pete* occasionally mentioned but not in detail. I need to run her name on our law enforcement database and see what we know."

Something fell to the floor from between the binding of the journal and its back cover as I lifted it off the table. I didn't notice any bulge there before. As I picked up the object, I was curious as I examined it. It looked like a quarter-sized, square-shaped golden dice, dotted with black circles all around, four dots on the edge of each side, one dot in the middle, a total of five on each side, except at the top and the bottom. Those had only one dot in the middle each. I tossed up the dice then caught it. It felt a bit heavy for a dice. Something was inscribed on one edge of the one-dotted sides. I squinted and read it: Isaiah 40:31.

"Hmm," I muttered, seeing it as very odd. Robert was engrossed in what he was reading, fingers working the pad, as he was busy taking notes, so I placed the cube on the table, planning to tell him about it later.

He turned to me suddenly. "Red, she took pretty detailed notes. It must have taken her a long time to put this together without getting caught in the process. The New Rulebook must be a first of its kind. It's lightyears ahead of anything I've heard of in surveillance technology." He paused in thought. Eyes glaringly fixed on one spot, a distant expression covered his face.

"You haven't heard the worst part yet. Apparently, The New Rulebook was developed both as leading technology in large-scale surveillance and as a means to control crime. It uses a system of mathematical probability and psychological logic coupled with past personal history to predict future behavior. It seeks to control crime through predicting a person's future behavior, using algorithms produced on the 'either/or' rules of probability and the 'if/then' rules of philosophical logic. Then it proposes a plan of action to stop that choice from actualization, if desired. That may sound like a load of crap to anyone on the street until they form a habit of crossing the street when the sign says Stop. The New Rulebook could propose cutting off their leg to prevent them from causing an accident. When it spotlights one individual, the true risk it poses becomes real enough. Why does anyone need something like this?"

He straightened, and his brows drew together. He turned his head sideways, lips thinning, eyes firmly set with displeasure, features rigidly drawn. "It could make anyone to be accused of anything at any time—depending on who's at the controls."

I considered him and his words for a moment, with my hand propping up my jaw as well. "For instance, if someone is poor, broke, and indebted, he's a prime candidate for theft suspicion automatically by virtue of his status."

He nodded in agreement. "That's not a fair assumption on their part. But, yes, that's what it means."

I shook my head. "That makes everyone a criminal before they even commit a crime. Right?"

He didn't nod this time. "Or you could be framed for a crime."

"Like I was," I completed, the full picture coming together—and not looking good for me. "That's how they chose me. I'm already a victim of The New Rulebook."

We were both silent for a while. He read a couple more pages. "From the looks of it, they were planning to go global with The New Rulebook. They just needed international corporations to sign on once the software is complete with the last ten percent."

I nodded. "That's where Violet comes in. Since they proceeded to kill her, we can assume she already developed it."

He rubbed his jaw. "You could be right. Maybe they just don't know where it is."

I sensed a spark in my mind's eye. So I picked up the cube, rolling it between my fingers. Then I tilted my jaw toward him. "What do you think this is? It fell out from inside the journal's binding." I extended it to him. Our fingers touched, and he pulled away quickly, looking more intensely at the object than I thought necessary. "Um—" I began. Then I thought twice about it. With regard to Robert, my imagination was probably starting to run away with me. I shrugged off my concern. "Never mind."

I rose to pour myself more coffee from the pot Robert had brewed. It was becoming harder to stave off sleep. Time was about two in the morning now. Considering that we'd arrived here at six last evening, that was a long time to have been working these details. "It looks like something she wanted to stay hidden—until it got into the right hands."

He flashed me a wide-eyed look, excitement dancing in his eyes. "Are you thinking what I'm thinking?"

Again, I nodded, setting my coffee cup quite some distance away from the cube this time. "It's like nothing I've ever seen. The inscription—"

"Yeah, I know the book of Isaiah chapter forty verse thirty-one says, we fly with wings as eagles and not get tired. Of course, I'm paraphrasing. I'll read from a Bible app on my phone."

I blinked then stared at him while he searched for his phone. "*You* have a Bible app? Since when?"

He kept searching intensely. But I knew he'd heard me. "There. Found it. So I'll read. Isaiah 40:31:

'Those who wait upon the Lord shall renew their strength; they shall mount up with wings as eagles; they shall run, and not be weary; they shall walk and not faint.'"

"What has that got to do with The New Rulebook?"

He rose and strolled to the window, straightening to full height. He stared at the dark night, arms crossed. "It means it's way bigger than we thought. The players are more powerful, more desperate than we imagine. To them, you're a loose end. They'll tear this city apart until they find you." He rubbed the back of his tense-looking neck, returning.

"Memorize as much as you can, anything you think is important. I'll do the same. We may part ways with this journal when we least expect." He turned around, face suddenly looking older.

My stomach churned, and I realized I hadn't eaten in several hours. In the interim, I reached for bottled water near my feet.

Robert settled into a seat next to me. "I need to raise this with my boss to loop him in. I'm sorry, but from the looks of it, we can't do this on our own anymore."

I rubbed my tired eyes, still lost in thought. "It's already morning. We can wait for a few hours. Then we go in."

He directed his gaze toward me, eyebrows arched high. "Remember, I'm on your side."

I smiled a little, knowing that was a given since I was framed. "I never doubted that. In the meantime, we need a math textbook, a philosophical logic text-book, a calculator, glue, a workbook, one roll of quarters, and a Polaroid camera."

He tipped his head sideways. "What for?"

I rose, pulling one of the throws along with me to the bedroom, my shoulders sunk in exhaustion. "I've got an idea. But for now, let's catch some sleep."

~

Natural light streamed in through the window, forcing its way through my eyelids. I groaned, the comfort of sleep still heavy on me. I tried to turn, only to hit the rugged side of a box next to me. At the obstruction, my eyelids flew open. Now fully awake, I took in my surroundings. Yes, now I remembered. I was in the new place Robert brought me to, which I still wasn't sure what or whose it was, but was intent on finding out when I wasn't running for my life. We'd arrived here yesterday evening and had been busy ever since. Soft linen cascaded down my arm as I flipped the blanket and picked up a note taped to the box. I rubbed my eyes to see the words clearly.

Morning, Ruby.

I'm at the precinct. There's some breakfast I ordered on the kitchen table. P.S. Please do not open the door to anyone who knocks. I've got keys.

I'll be back soonest,

Robert.

I grew still and could hardly believe I was all

alone. I set the note aside and glanced at it. Where did I begin? I rose and opened the shoebox. It contained everything Robert and I had stayed up late, well into the wee hours of the morning, drawing up. Plans, test running ideas, and possible scenarios. Every scrap piece we jotted down and drew on was inside. I rummaged through to the bottom of the box, exhaling when I touched the leather-bound journal Violet Zendel had given me.

I put the box down and rose to my feet. It certainly felt like more than a day has passed since then, thanks to the events that occurred. The little sleep I'd gotten seemed to have done me some good at least. The headache had all but disappeared, though I still felt a bit sore.

I made my way to the bathroom and pushed the door open. Now aided by daylight, I saw it was more spacious than the one I'd minimally cleaned up at on our way here. A new set of bath soap, unopened toothbrush, and tiny toothpaste lined the upper shelf by the wall.

They were bare basic amenities, but I was truly grateful for them right now. I wrapped my hair up inside a shower cap. I looked down and saw myself still clad in the long shirt—the length of a robe—Robert had given me early this morning when I was about to sleep. Before he offered to sleep on the couch while I took the bedroom. This wasn't the first of the few times we'd shared general unisex clothing, but it was the first time it happened since we left the orphanage. After slipping out of the long shirt, I stepped into the bathtub, and a velvety rain of warmth showered my worn body.

~

Afterward, I put on the white tee and blue jeans I'd managed to squeeze into the duffel bag. I walked back into the bedroom then lifted the duffel bag onto the bed, ready to organize the items. Something fell to the ground. I looked, and it was a business card. I picked it up and read: Alex Wexler. Just then, everything felt raw and real all of a sudden. I remembered Alex. He was a son to one of my elderly neighbors on the second floor who owned a beauty supply store I sometimes patronized.

Tears welled up in my eyes. I may never see these people again. I'd enjoyed working with them so much, that the weight of loss bore heavily on my shoulders. ... I sat down, holding the card like it was a piece of my soul that had been torn away from me. These people, they'd given me a chance and had believed in me when no one else would.

That was how I started my business. Armed with high school diplomas, Robert and I had no money for college. Robert played soccer, so he went to community college and earned an Associates' Degree. I followed a year later. But money was tight. I had to work three jobs to get through those two years. It wasn't easy for Robert either. Whatever we had, we shared. There was no time for leisure or entertainment. We had only one shot. We both graduated, and finding a professional well-paying job was tough.

Almost as soon as he graduated, Robert joined the police, and we split his first paycheck right down the middle, to get me a place to live. We found an apartment building in a suburb where everyone was aged above sixty—except myself and the owner who inherited the building from his late parents.

I'd thanked Robert. Then I cried for two straight days. I promised myself I'd never be a financial burden to him again. I'd find a job even if it meant flipping burgers.

When I finally worked up the courage to step out of the apartment on my third day, all my neighbors greeted me with a wonderful and surprising warmth. On my way home with a small bag of groceries, an elderly lady approached while I waited for the elevator. She smiled, asking if I could please assist her in purchasing some bread, milk, and eggs because her knees were hurting really bad that day.

I said sure without hesitation. She then added that her friend upstairs could use my help as well, if I wouldn't mind. So I agreed. We went up there together, and her friend was thrilled, offering me fifteen dollars for my services. Her friend even suggested I could pick up some groceries for myself on her tab. An offer I politely declined.

But it took me a moment to realize what had just happened. An opportunity was born for me. After making the deliveries, I asked the ladies to inform me when next they needed supplies. The charge would be a ten-dollar flat fee, so there was no need to bid for my services. They agreed, and I started making weekly deliveries. Next, I walked down to the library and made a flyer for my business, posting it in the building's lounge area and wondering if anyone would even bother reading it. But they surprised me in a good way.

Within two weeks, I had more customers, and with them, came free publicity. So I put up a pinned board, along with a purse hidden behind it, held with a hook onto my front door. Every morning, patrons, also neighbors, appended their names to the board and attached a note containing their shopping list. Payments and tips went into the purse behind the board.

I registered for and completed a class on delivery services, earned a certificate, and then filed with the state for a license.

When I told Robert, he was skeptical. But when he saw that I was serious, he backed down and began to support me. That was something we'd decided when we were much younger. We would respect each other's boundaries—especially when we didn't agree.

Soon I made between seven to eight hundred dollars a week, including tips, weather permitting. I offered Robert back the money he'd paid for my first rent. In response, he didn't speak to me for a week until I apologized and retracted the offer. So I saved the money.

Moving forward, I expanded my business, reaching out to other seniors' homes, placing ads in newspapers, even cold-calling private companies. It was tough at first, getting them to trust me, but I was armed with recommendations from my current customers. Others who were outside that circle came slowly. The need was more important to them, and I ensured that I never broke their trust.

I was excited, and I worked very hard too. Then businesses and offices started calling me and asking for my services in delivering documents and parcels. My lower fees and same-day across-town services drew them away from patronizing the name-brand companies with their long waiting periods. I began to rent a car daily then saved up to buy a small car for delivery.

I could hardly believe my success. Before long, my elderly customers were recommending my services to their sons and daughters, who ranked high on the corporate ladder in huge companies. Last week, I'd started searching for an assistant right before I received the request for yesterday's delivery, in an area under renovation due to damage from tornado-strength winds last fall.

So I'd surmised that it must have been a construction company. Construction companies were some of my highest paying customers because they usually needed fast deliveries. I assumed they'd offered such a high price due to the need for speedy delivery and the item's importance. Of course, no amount of money was worth my good name and my innocence was not for sale, but they had definitely underpaid me by a very wide margin!

When I'd arrived a couple minutes early, I saw the lady was an early bird too.

I *did* wonder what delivery could be important enough for someone to pay me ten thousand bucks to pick up. But companies had paid me something close to that amount before, so I didn't question it.

I sighed, crossing to the kitchen area to fix something to eat, though I doubted I had any appetite. I opened several kitchen cabinets and eyed the canned food. Sighting an instant macaroni & cheese packet, I carefully pulled it out. I placed a small pot on the stove, adding some water into it. I guessed that Robert would also need to eat something when he got back before we left for the station together—to whatever awaited me there.

∼

An hour later, Robert walked through the door. Though the time was barely eleven in the morning, his shoulders drooped, his face was long, and his eyes lacked their usual spark. I could hardly believe how far he was willing to go to assist me, even though we hadn't seen each other much lately. A twinge squeezed my heart. How many times did I choose not to spend time with him since my business picked up speed? And all the while, he'd been a true friend.

"Robert, you know how much I like kitchen duty, right?" I laced the words with enough sarcasm.

He nodded. "Yeah, like you love being chased

across town by unknown bad guys." A glint brightened his eyes.

"Good. I made you some macaroni and cheese. It's in the fridge if you're hungry, just pop it in the microwave."

He looked up with surprise inching up his brow. "Red, you cooked for me? No way! I'm definitely eating that."

I chuckled, glad that he'd cheered up. I was also glad I'd cooked something instead of sitting on my hands.

He strode halfway to the kitchen when his phone rang. He pulled it from his pocket, flipping it open. Seconds passed while he listened. "Sure. No problem. Tell him I'll be right back. Okay, I'll bring her along. Bye."

"Who was that and who is *her*?"

But he didn't answer immediately. Instead, he dashed across the room and grabbed his coat. He picked up the leather-bound journal and handed it to me. "We got to hurry. They could already be on their way here. I'll explain in the rented car." He lifted up the duffel bag and strode briskly toward the door.

"Robert, what's going on? Have we been made?" I asked, a pitch higher than when the conversation was about food.

He pointed to the clock on the wall behind him, facing me. "What exact time is it?"

"It's ten forty-nine a.m." What did the call have to do with the time? "Robert, are we in danger?"

He laced his shoes. "I have thirty seconds to answer, and then we leave immediately."

I straightened. "Okay. I'm listening."

"On second thought, I think we should leave everything here." When I yielded the journal, he accepted it then tucked it inside the duffel bag.

I zipped it up, opting to hide it inside a large kitchen cabinet instead.

"I think they connected you and me in this thing. Someone from the station called and asked where I am. But I didn't tell him. He said my boss wants me to come in right away. The problem is I didn't tell anyone I had left. I'm supposed to be on early lunch in a few minutes' time. If someone's looking into me, trying to find you, they'll simply time the period between when they called me and when I arrive at the station, and then triangulate the search grid for you."

I slipped on my shoes while he spoke to hasten our exit. "Then I should definitely go with you."

He now hesitated. "You're right, we should go together. Just speculating, but...what if no one's tied me to you yet? You could be safer here. But if it takes me the same drive time to get back, and they've linked us both, they'll find you before sunset even if you stay behind."

I nodded in agreement. "So we get there faster and beat the clock."

But he shook his head. "Actually, we'll be there in nine minutes instead of thirty. I need this location to remain very secure for us."

There was no time to ask him why. I pulled my

hair into a hard bun with a rubber band on my arm, grabbed some bottled water while he picked up the duffel bag once more. "Go, Robert!"

We dashed to the door, but he stopped, regarding me quizzically. "Wait, where's the die?"

I pointed to the side. "I've got it." He stared at me, so I explained, "It's hidden in my earring. Don't ask." I prodded him through the front door, following right at his heels.

"Robert, we've got eight minutes and ten seconds." As the time whittled down, we raced down the stairs.

"Got it."

When we reached the bottom of the stairs and approached the outer door, I froze on the spot. I couldn't move. My last experience at the base of a stairwell flashed back and held me in place. I heard Robert, but he sounded far away. Within moments, I was hyperventilating, and I felt powerless to stop it. With one hand, I gripped the stair railing for support.

"Red, take a deep breath. It will pass. Deep breath, okay?"

To my relief, I heard him clearly now. I nervously proceeded with a step. Then I took another. I held Robert's hand tightly as we walked through the doors. This time, thankfully, uneventfully.

As we exited, I squinted against the bright sunlight, searching for his car while he fumbled in his pocket for the keys. Several cars were lined up on the side of the street. I spotted one with a rental car logo three cars over and took a step.

Then I grabbed his hand and pointed at the side. "There's a camera."

So we kept our heads down while making our way to the car.

Entering his car, we buckled up fast. "Hurry, but please avoid the traffic cameras, Robert."

He nodded, casting me a worried glance.

I smiled weakly. "I'm fine, don't worry. Thank you for helping me out back there, but now, you've got to keep your eyes on the road. We have six minutes."

With a curt nod, he started the car and roared its engine, and we drove off. Unknown to him, I was still scared, so I hid my still trembling hands between my thighs, crossing them and wishing that things didn't get worse.

∼

Upon our arrival, the sun shone brightly overhead as we walked through the doors of the Windstar mega-building in Silver Stone, housing the Metropolitan Police Department. Without effort, we blended into the lunch-hour pedestrian flow. Aromas from strangers' lunch packages assaulted my nostrils, bringing memories of a home-cooked meal and sending hungry churns down my stomach. Neither Robert nor I had gotten to eat the ready-to-eat meal I'd cooked. The inviting aroma around now became bittersweet—as an unwanted reminder of being forced to leave home unwillingly.

Robert loosely took my hand, still looking straight

ahead. "Don't look, but behind us, to your left, there are two men—one tall, one short—coming out of a parked car up front. They seem to be searching people's faces. I'm not sure, but they might be the bad guys looking for you."

Involuntarily, my grip tightened.

"Relax. We'll detour in three, two, one." We turned a sharp right corner, heading toward an exit marked Stairs. Robert strode ahead, pushed the large door inward, and held it open as I walked through. He cast one more glance behind us then hurried the door shut, though it could have closed automatically. "I'm just making sure we weren't followed," he answered my unasked question.

I smiled then, knowing I'd been right. With Robert and me, few words sufficed.

We made our way onto the second floor then walked through a set of double doors on the right marked Metropolitan Police Department.

I swallowed hard, although I wasn't exactly sure what kind of welcome awaited me. My guess was that it would be a handshake or cuffs. Officers rushed by us with papers threatening to fly from their hands. A middle-aged woman walking with a cane complained to an officer that she was wrongfully pulled over and cited. A young lady seated near an open door seemed unperturbed by her cuffed hands, chewing gum loudly. An elderly couple sat near the entrance, coffee cup in hand, while reading newspapers, appearing relaxed. Robert kept holding my hand. Though I thought to tug free when we entered, somehow I held on. I needed the support his hand provided me right now.

With a warm smile, he greeted those officers we passed by. One of them winked at him after casting me a curious glance.

"Okay, Robert, we need to hurry it up here."

He smiled but didn't seem to be in a hurry. "Are you afraid of all the admirable attention you're getting, Red? Relax, they're harmless."

I pressed my lips together. "This is serious. My life's on the line here. I can't just breeze through a police station when I've been framed for a crime."

He stopped, gazing at me with a strange confidence. "Exactly. The operative word being 'framed'. You were the one who always says to live in freedom every moment. Plus, with the 'gift' they left you at the window in your apartment, I'm pretty sure they wouldn't do that if you weren't innocent. So, I suggest we take this one step at a time until we find these guys. Don't lose who you truly are. Keep them out of that pretty head o' yours. The moment they get you to start thinking like you would if you did it, they've gotten you." He craned his neck out, eyebrows arched high, waiting for my response.

I sighed, looking past ahead. "Okay. Okay."

We zipped through the waiting area, slowing at the end of the hallway. Then we stopped at a desk marked Detective Towers. For the first time since we entered the MPD, a huge smile spread across my face. "Oh yeah. Let's see what we've got here...."

One look at me, then at the desk, and his face

flushed red. Robert scrambled. "Red! Please don't say it."

My hands planted firmly on my hips. "Oh no, Robert. I promise you, there's no way I'm missing out on this." I reached out, grabbing his cell phone from his pocket before he protested. "But first, let me take a picture to immortalize this moment."

While I clicked away at random speed, he tried to move things away quickly before I was done, but I'd captured sufficient disorganization.

"I won the bet. You owe me two hundred bucks. Pay up." I laughed as sweat beads formed on his forehead and he sulked.

We'd set this bet two years ago when we celebrated his new job, and he'd said then that "for a hundred bucks per annum, I'll never have a messy desk." From the orphanage, I knew he organized everything well—especially his wardrobe—but never papers. So playfully, I'd accepted the bet. Now, I raised the phone, pressing the camera one more time to capture his nervous face.

"You're having jitters over this? Aren't you supposed to be more fit than—" Flashing red lights dotted the top edge of the camera's view bouncing reflectively off the monitor screen. I hadn't seen them earlier. I tapped my fingers to zoom in. But it was now flashing faster, in quick succession. There wasn't enough time.

"Robert!" I shouted. Then I grabbed his arm and pushed him to the ground and into an opposite cubicle. A pinging sound pierced through.

"What is it?" he asked as we rose to our feet moments later, panting.

"I saw something, like a flash of light. It moved like...laser beams." Everyone else seemed preoccupied with what they were doing. No one even glanced toward us. We approached cautiously. A thin film of smoke rose from the left part of the seat as a burning smell stained the air.

A hole was torn into his seat—right where his heart would've been. There was no way he would have seen it if he was sitting down. Until it was too late. We stared at each other while Robert's jaw slacked and his eyeballs rounded in shock. As I looked away, my eyes trailed black soot lining the cream-colored wall, showing the trajectory of the laser-like beam.

"They now know you're with me." The words tumbled out of his lips heavily.

He straightened, took my arm, and headed us back in the direction we came, at a rapid pace, all smiles gone. "Yeah. It also means we're no longer safe here." We made our way down the stairs through the main exit and out of the MPD, also known as the SSPD.

5

HE GUIDES ME IN THE PATHS OF RIGHTEOUSNESS FOR HIS name's sake... -Psalm 23:3

"Y ou two should have stayed off the cameras," a grainy voice said from behind us. "Don't bother trying to run."

We whisked around. Robert raised a hand to his belt out of habit. But his weapon wasn't there. He'd lost them at Ms. Bryant's place as we fled. He'd told me he'd filed it as missing this morning at the station, reporting everything I told him, too—including what happened at my apartment—to his boss, who then asked to see me immediately. That was why we came in.

Two men now accosted us, one was tall with grim eyes, the other one was short with rough-looking hair dropping down his face. They had to be the two men

Robert warned me about when we arrived at the MPD.

"Excuse me, who are you?" I asked, knowing the implication if my suspicion was right.

"Well, aren't you back from the dead? I didn't expect you to survive your window suicide. You must have had some kind of luck." The tall one grinned and looked me over with cold eyes. With a hand pressed against my back, he shoved me forward.

"I guess your luck just ran out, missy," the short man added, blowing a wisp of matted hair off his face. Resentment seethed through his eyes.

Robert refused to move. The huge man's deep-set eyes flew toward Robert impatiently. "Listen, man, I've got a gun to your back. You want me to use it on you...*here?*"

Robert hesitated. Then our eyes met so I nodded. In compliance, he began to move.

"Smart choice." The other man remained close behind the three of us as we exited the Windstar building, held captive.

～

Both men led us toward a semi-covered parking lot, on the first parking level. Lighting was dim and barely enough to see with. As we approached a turn, two officers handed out flyers.

The tall man's grip on my back tightened. "All smiles. No games."

I knew what he meant.

"Hello, ma'am, how are you doing today?" The first officer bowed a little.

So I smiled. "All right, thank you, officer."

The officer waved to Robert also in uniform, but he stood some yards away with the short man, who nodded in return. "We're having the MPD Christian Fellowship's in-house concert this afternoon. We'd love to have you there. Everyone's invited." He turned to Robert. "Hey, buddy, I thought I saw you at the last fellowship? You can bring your friends."

Robert cast me a glance, and I gaped at him. "Yeah, I was there with a colleague. Sorry, I can't make it today. But thank you, though," he replied with his eyes still fixed on me.

I faced away. Clearly, I didn't know *that* happened. Robert was getting serious with religion?

The other officer smiled broadly toward me, observing nothing strange. I guessed he was probably just glad the temperatures were up today for a change this spring. He handed me a flyer so I accepted it. "Oh no, lady! It's not old folks like me who would be singing. I sound more like a frog's croak when I try."

We all laughed, starting with the man with a gun to Robert's back, then the one with a harsh hand on mine. It dawned on me that these officers might be the last people to see us alive. My lips began to tremble. But I couldn't really show them the seriousness of our predicament. If I tried an escape, the armed man could shoot both of them within seconds. So I smiled a little instead, while I still could.

"Thank you very much, officer. We appreciate your invitation." I tucked the flyer into my pocket as we strode past them into the garage, their happy chatter lingering on my mind as my last specks of hope began to disappear.

~

"Y**ou're** going in separate vehicles." A rough arm tore between us as Robert and I tried to stay close. We approached their truck parked in an obscure corner of the parking lot.

Robert halted. "Why?"

The man shoved him forward. "Why? Because I've got my orders, just like you cops get yours."

Robert held up a hand. "Wait. Before we go, can I say goodbye?"

The huge man hesitated, while the other sighed, followed by a frown.

"She's my best friend. We've known each other for eighteen years. Can I *please* say goodbye?"

The huge man nodded toward me. "Two minutes."

The other man argued with him as Robert left them and drew closer to me. He hugged me and leaned in, his mouth plastered to my ear. "Red, you were right, and I'm really sorry. There are two things I haven't told you. I've been hoping for the right time and place, but so far..." His shoulders slacked.

I looked at him, but he leaned in close again, ready tears brimming in his eyes. Robert was not one to cry. *I* did the crying. So, whatever it was, it had to be

tougher than our present situation. I braced myself
for the news.

"I'm now a Christian...since two weeks ago. It's still
all very new to me, but it's been quite an experience."
He paused, letting his revelation sink in. "And I'm now
in love with you, Red. Very much so."

Then, I gasped, not sure which news shocked me
more. I suppose the second one since it had more to
do with me. I cared deeply about Robert, but a new
faith was one thing, being in love with me? That was a
whole other issue! What was I supposed to think? I
turned away, searching for an escape, the news too
much to take in all at once. Instead, I slammed right
into him losing my balance.

He caught me by the waist, steadying me while
drawing me close. His green eyes stared into mine
then lowered eagerly to my lips. He blushed deeply
up to his ears, his desire for me unhidden.

I tore away, pointing a finger at him while shaking
my head vigorously. "Not you, Robert! No!" I rushed
forward, away from him, and the men speedily
approached, bounding fast.

I closed my eyes momentarily. "How did this
happen?" How did I miss the signs?

Robert stepped up behind me. "Red! I don't know
how it happened, I promise."

I froze then flipped around. "But you know *when* it
happened?" I wished to hear that this was all a mix-
up, created by the current circumstances.

"Red..." His voice sounded high-pitched. Then I
knew.

My hand flew up before I spoke. "No. Robert Towers. My name is Ruby. Stick with that. Now, when?" My chest rose and fell with every syllable, the hurt and loss already rising inside me and waiting to bubble over. I knew what he was going to say now even before the words came. He'd never lied to me. I loathed how I knew that he was telling the truth. I shut my eyes again as the men neared us, their voices rising, but I didn't hear them. I listened for the one voice I'd recognize anywhere, even asleep. I heard his breath go still.

"The Unique...when you danced. I couldn't—"

But I wasn't listening anymore. I'd just lost the only person I ever truly had.

~

"Orders have changed. We're taking you two together," the huge man announced. "Move." He shooed Robert and me into one truck, oblivious to our turmoil. But we followed without a word. The truck looked very odd. No license plates showed as far as I could see.

It had unusually high clearance from the ground. The driver's section seemed longer than most, and the back was like a box attached to it. He pressed a button on his keychain, and the back slid open, steel panes separating them, one upward, the other downward. Steps dropped from the sides, and he set the first one to the ground, testing. "Get in."

We followed without question. I hadn't even

thrown Robert a glance since our latest interaction. It was better that way. I needed some breathing room, and this box of a truck we were in felt too small right now.

We were set on what looked like airplane cargo seats. A lock automatically snapped into place. Our hands were tied behind our backs, while our feet were secured. The fellowship flyer I'd received fell from my pocket to the ground.

"It doesn't open without these keys." The huge man jiggled his keychain in warning, walking away, out of the box. Robert and I sat face to face across from each other.

"You got any last words?" The short man laughed, peering into my face, his rough hair dangled in front, while his stained teeth made me wish he didn't open his mouth. If crankiness had a face, this was it.

Both men exited the box, slamming the doors shut. Their footsteps scuffled on the cement as they headed to the front of the truck. Dim light was our only companion, alternated by jiggling empty beer cans falling on each other as the men started the truck and moved without warning. Then my ride to oblivion began.

We'd been riding for what felt like an eternity, though it could have been only an hour. It gave us plenty of time to think. I avoided Robert's gaze. I didn't remember us being this silent in eighteen years. It'd been eighteen years since we met. In frustration, my eyes teared up, and my heart filled with every kind of emotion as I traveled back in time.

At the time, we were both six. I had been in the orphanage for maybe a couple of weeks. I'd seen Robert a few times in the cafeteria, but we didn't speak. He glanced at me more than once—when I cared to look up from a book I read. He was the kind of person who made everyone laugh around him. But I figured I was not his type of friend. Younger kids followed him around, often snacking on treats he gladly shared. I had neither treats nor a towering height so I felt I didn't belong.

One afternoon during lunch, a kid bumped my shoulder, causing my water cup to spill. Another kid moving fast—known to be a bully—slipped on the spill and landed on the ground with a thud. It's funny how I don't recall his name.

He cursed at me, rose with fury-filled eyes, and knocked over the rest of my lunch tray. Everything stopped. Everyone's eyes fastened on both of us. Then the chants began. Chants for a duel. I'd never fought before. I wasn't interested either. But the chants were insistent. I doubted I could just leave.

The bully sunk a foot into the food mess, but I didn't move. I'd seen him give some kids a black eye. Many were scared of him. I was not. I stood my ground, yet without saying a word. His breath reeked of garlic—evidence that he'd sneaked pizza from the staff luncheon. That emboldened me further. We were now inches apart. The chants rose higher, plates clanging on the tables now. Arms firmly planted on my hips, I stepped closer. Then they all stopped, waiting.

"I won't hit you. I'm classy."

Cheers erupted. Some banged their plates on the dining table in support of me.

I whirled around, picked up my dropped plate, and began walking away. A couple of steps later, I heard some ruckus behind me so I turned sharply. Robert had tackled the bully to the ground.

Another boy—aged about three and one of Robert's little friends—came to me. He looked up. "He was coming at you with a plate. Big Rob jumped in then got hit in the head himself."

My hands flew to my mouth. Here was this kid I hardly knew, taking blows for me. Within a full minute, both boys were well mired in my lunch. Robert rose, stopped in front of me, and then walked away without a word, toward the boys' bathroom. The bully still roiled on the ground, rubbing his eyes, apparently unable to see well. I seized the chance to get away, tossing my plate in the bin. I went after Robert, hoping to catch him outside the restroom before he entered, to thank him.

But I'd arrived too late. So I leaned on a large pillar between the boys' and girls' restrooms, waiting. No one else was around.

"You've got someone fighting for you, huh?" a scruffy voice said.

I whisked toward the voice.

The bully emerged from the shadows, his face still a mess, eyes red and puffy—for a change.

There, alone with him, my heart flew to my mouth. I tried not to show it. He was older, taller too. He only needed to punch me a few times to put me out for hours, if not days. Somehow, I remained unafraid.

"You made me look bad." He flexed his fingers threateningly. "I'll show you."

"Well, I'm not sure how beating me to a pulp in front of the restroom will redeem your image. I don't see anyone else around," I countered. I wasn't even sure he understood what "pulp" meant anyway. Thanks to the educative cartoon pamphlets I'd been reading, I had lots of words to play around with.

The laughter and chatter of kids leaving the cafeteria filtered out. I placed my hands on my waist, hoping to scare him away.

It didn't work since he didn't budge. Instead, he raised a balled fist.

"Leave her alone," someone bellowed.

The bully froze.

I turned to the opposite side toward the voice. It was Robert. His face had turned pink, and his fist was curled into a ball. He stepped in between the bully and me. He looked fierce but cute.

"I said," he spoke with emphasis, "walk away."

The boy must've sensed that Robert meant every word. He was older, but Robert was more determined. And he sounded like he could beat him up if he wanted to. The bully stepped back, waved his hands in the air, with a bruised ego stamped on his face. "I've never seen vanilla fighting for chocolate."

Those words were filled with enough racial tinge, I could taste it from where I was. I whirled toward him, defiant. "Who told you I need someone to fight for me?"

The bully stared at us then rubbed his swollen eyes.

"I can make your eyes worse if you want," Robert said, like adding salt to injury.

"I'll get you someday." The bully's nose now ran with mucus.

Neither of us spoke. Then he walked away. Relieved, I turned to Robert. That was our first time alone together. First time I noticed his emerald-green sparkling eyes. I stared into them, and he stared into mine. But it didn't feel weird at all. Strangely, we felt comfortable in each other's company.

"Why did you fight for me?" I was not sure what he expected in return.

He extended me a hand. "To be friends."

I frowned. Did he read my mind? "I'm sorry. I didn't—"

He cut in. The first of many times in future he'd do so. "I'd like us to be friends if you don't mind."

Friendship? That's why he got beat up for me?

We shook hands. "Sure. Let's be friends."

We both smiled. "But on one condition though, we don't talk about—"

He cut in again, "Deal. Sorry he said vanilla, chocolate..." He feigned the bully's tone, and we laughed heartily. "Now I want some ice cream because of what he said." We made our way back to the cafeteria, feeling lighthearted. "Vanilla or chocolate?" I looked at him quizzically. "Both, of course." He smiled. "Me too." From then on, we became inseparable. We watched each other's back. I loved apples, but he hated them. So I ate his and my share, while he would eat half my sandwich because I hated green leaves of any kind. His little friends became my friends too. After we both grew older and left the orphanage, time became an issue. He was engrossed in his studies, and I in mine. We made effort each week to speak on the phone.

After community college, my business took off. We initially planned to get together for lunch every weekend, but after two weekends, we began to postpone—time constraints again. We talked every couple of weeks, but they were always hurried conversations. Despite the growing physical distance, Robert never compromised on calling me on my birthday and spending all day Christmas Day with me. We planned ahead, so the entire day was booked with fun activities.

Friends came and went in our lives, one or two boyfriends for me and some girlfriends for him too, but we remained there for each other. I never asked him about his parentage. He never asked about mine. I think we both knew it wouldn't change our circumstances, and so we didn't bother.

He'd said he had a huge surprise planned for my

birthday this year. I wasn't sure what it was, but I'd been looking forward to it. Well, now it didn't matter anymore. I'd be lucky to make my birthday coming up in a few weeks. Actually, from the danger we now faced, I'd be lucky to make it through today.

A jolt on a rough patch brought me back to the moment. Robert was staring at me—in a kind way, so I smiled.

He smiled back. "Your face was...You okay?"

His cheeks had sunk in deeper, no thanks to our present circumstances. I nodded in response. "Yeah."

He bowed his head a little. "Good."

I should say something—something generic to bridge our growing gap. "I'm surprised they put us in here together. Weren't they scared that we'd try to escape?"

He shrugged. "They heard our voices going earlier."

I quickly turned away. There was no need for the reminder—especially now. When I turned again, he was still watching keenly. "I've got to ask you something, Robert."

His lashes inched up. "Of course. Shoot."

I drew in a deep breath and hoped to frame my thoughts into the right words. "We're already best friends. Why ruin it? There's nothing about each other we don't know."

His gaze remained steady, though softening. "Not everything."

It took a moment for what he referenced to settle in my mind. Then heat rose to my neck, but I didn't budge. "You know what I mean, everything else without intimacy."

His lips pressed together, and color filled his cheeks. "Still doesn't change how I now feel about you. I'm not going to hide it either. I couldn't even if I tried because you know me better than anyone else."

Yeah, it was going to be right in my face for a while I thought, and then wished I hadn't.

Suddenly, I began to imagine how hard it must have been for him to keep it from me for however long. Everything slowly began to make sense. Like when he'd pulled his hands away when they touched mine last night. Little things that didn't fit before were now clear. I still didn't know how I missed the signs. Now we were here. At the back of a truck heading to God knows where.

This space now felt even smaller. I sighed. "I apologize for my reaction earlier. It was...totally shocking news. I needed a moment to take it all in. I can say it was also bad timing. I need to process what's happening to me, to my life. Everything I've worked hard for is being torn from me by some...ghost. I'm deep in the ocean here. You've been like my safe place, Robert. I don't need a storm right now. So please just...wait for a better time to talk about this."

Another jolt from the vehicle landed my behind on hard mid-seat dividers, sending a wave through my spine. I returned my focus to the conversation. We hadn't talked about Robert's conversion to Christianity. I wasn't sure that I was ready to do so right now.

He rubbed his chin with a raised angled knee, then sat up straight again. "The family that lives across from my apartment are having a party right now for their three-year-old daughter's birthday. Our investigations' team is having a meeting at the moment, and they don't even know I've been abducted. Your clients are probably worried sick since not reaching you for two straight days. How do those elderly women get supplies when they run out? There are so many other places we could—in fact, should— be right now. But we're here. Against our will. Ruby, what you call bad timing could be perfect timing for God. No matter what happens at the destination, you don't give them anything. Please, or all we've gone through would be for nothing."

The truck suddenly halted. Robert shook his restraints, but they didn't budge. He glanced up at me, a frown lining his forehead. "If you see a chance of escape, take it."

I nodded. "You do the same."

The front doors clicked open then slammed shut. Footsteps crunched on rough ground toward the rear of the truck.

Robert inched forward, his eyes wild, and seeming more desperate than I'd seen before. "Please do what I'm about to ask. If you ever get to your last straw, call on the name of Jesus. He will help you. I'm not trying to convert you. I'm only giving you hope. It's worked for me."

I hesitated because this was new ground.

"Please, Red. Promise me." His voice and eyes pleaded.

He just called me Red, after I'd asked him not to do so again. I inhaled deeply. The men began unlocking the latch. We had mere seconds to finish this conversation. "Okay, Robert. I'll keep it in mind."

He exhaled, his shoulders relaxing as he leaned back. "That works—for now. Thank you."

The doors slid open. Bright daylight streamed in, stunning my eyes. I blinked a couple of times, adjusting to the brightness. My feet felt as though they were held with lead. The short man entered and silently released my ankles from the restraints, leading me out. As my shoes touched the ground, the tall man followed, bringing Robert behind. The fragrance of roses in full bloom filtered into my nostrils. Then came the whoosh like a taking-off plane.

I looked around and was so stunned that I could hardly believe my eyes. "Wow."

6
_____

Cortexe Corp. Park boldly inscribed a white marble block structure, hemmed around by a garden. White and red roses, bleeding hearts, and agaves tumbled over the partition on all sides. Farther away stood an architectural masterpiece many stories high, with an electronic screen flashing the name *Cortexe Corp.* at the uppermost tip and blocking direct sunlight. Below the company name was another inscription, "Rule the world with a click". A forefinger pointed skyward. The few windows around the huge building were strangely blocked with iron bars and painted white.

People passed by and went about their normal business. I walked on paved ground as we approached the building. A few cast us curious glances, but most simply hurried along. When we got closer, I noticed several smaller buildings dotting the campus-structured landscape, all linked by paved roads to the main building like arms to a monster. They were pretty outside but ugly inside.

A group of men approached us, all clothed in black wear, heavily armed, and looking rugged. They clutched their weapons tightly, and their narrow eyes darted back and forth as if Robert and I had come with an army. They met up with us, then turned and escorted us inside. We were led through huge opaque glass doors, towering at least twelve feet tall. Red lights positioned at eye level on the doors blinked continuously the moment we swung through.

Veering sharply to the left, we entered a transparent elevator—resembling a portal. The elevator moved up, and then suddenly slid sideways toward a cube-shaped structure, stopping on a walkway. Black dots marked the sides.

I gasped at the sight. Four dots were on each edge, and one occupied the center. They were the same as the cube hidden inside my earring! I directed my gaze at Robert then caught his quick glance. Clearly, he'd seen the resemblance too.

We stepped off the elevator onto the walkway platform, and it clicked beneath my shoes. Although it appeared to be metal, it didn't feel metallic. It felt more like a sheet, but a strong one with a firm grip on one's shoe soles. Its grip clung so tightly that it was impossible to run on it. Then I thought maybe that was the intent. As we waited for another elevator at the end of the platform, I recalled the view from outside.

This place was a small city in the middle of nowhere—one with a private airstrip. No other building was visible as far as I could see. *And* it had portal-like elevators, which left me wondering, who built this? Who owned Cortexe Corp.?

Elevator doors chimed and opened, interrupting my thoughts. We entered it, and the huge man pressed an X button on the elevator. The buttons for each floor were not numbers, but instead, they were scientific symbols—Alpha, Beta, Function, then X.

I gulped down the worries threatening to swallow me. On top of that, X was not a scientific symbol.

Just then, we emerged into a brightly colored room. "Wait here," the huge man ordered, so we stopped.

The short man stepped in between Robert and me, with one hand on his weapon. Robert had been silent all this while, but I knew his brain wasn't. I longed to say something kind to him, anything to relax his visibly taut shoulders, something I knew he needed to hear. But I didn't. Instead, I just stood there, feeling helpless. He closed his eyes meditatively, and I figured he was probably praying. This was all new territory because I'd never seen him do anything remotely similar. Granted, we attended Sunday school back at the orphanage once a month—only the Sundays when they served candies. But it was nothing serious like this.

The huge man returned and opened doors to what appeared to be an office, only wider. "Get in."

We complied, and as we entered, I saw several people thumbing away at computers, seeming as busy as ants. They were all dressed in similar uniform— black pants and white shirts. There were at least three rows of them, sitting at openly viewable desks set next to each other. The floors and ceiling were well lit, shining brightly. So did the walls. But I saw no windows. Rather than having windows, a large screen was set on the wall, and it was scrolling through data I couldn't decipher.

"Belly of the beast," I caught Robert's murmur.

In response, the huge guy shoved him forward. "Get down to the back." We passed all those people, but they were so engrossed that they barely noticed us.

"Speed it up, Mark. We need that to correspond," someone instructed among the feverish-fingered workers. The guy being ordered to work was barely in his early twenties. So I wondered, who were these people? What were they doing here—in a building the exact shape as the die hidden in one of my earrings?

We reached the back, pausing in front of a door with a sign, Caution Do Not Enter. One of the men stood at a random-looking spot, and a thumb pad emerged from the wall in front of him.

"Say or enter your authorization code," a voice from the pad instructed.

He stared at a tiny piece of paper he'd pulled from

his pocket. "H-1-5-9-Z," the man opted to say. And the walls parted in circular motion leading to an inner room.

"Come on in. Feel at home," someone lazily said from inside.

But I refused to move.

"He said move!" the short man barked at me, clearly a bit too eager to let out the pent-up animosity I'd noticed when they'd first accosted us.

I obliged, though unwillingly.

We all stepped in without further delay. I looked behind. The wall-like doors slid firmly shut behind us while a laser beam came on over the spot we'd entered through. I whisked around, keenly scanning the room. Smoke from the butt of a half-smoked cigar rose lazily to the ceiling near the room's center. Robert sneezed in reaction to the taint of smoke.

Someone occupying a black leather swivel chair swung it around to face us. A monitor hung over the far wall displayed the workers we'd encountered in the previous room. Another screen showed the front of a room with wide steel doors. A digital security lock jutted out from the door, and one armed guard stood in front of it.

The man rose and approached us. He was bald at the center, and he had a sheepish grin, like a kid who'd gotten lucky in Scrabble. He clapped his hands together. "So! Shall we?" He pulled two adjacent chairs forward. "Please. Sit."

Robert and I glided into the seats without a choice.

He got in Robert's face first, his grin noticeably wider. "Welcome to Cortexe Corp. headquarters, Detective Robert Towers. By the way, congratulations on your recent promotion."

Robert blinked at him, oblivious to what he was referencing.

"Oh, you don't know yet, do you? I forgot to mention that your boss approved your promotion this afternoon. You're now Sergeant. Too bad you won't be there to receive it." He rubbed his palms together again, his mouth grinning wider. "I bet you want to know why we made you take this trip out to paradise, huh?"

Wait, did he just say...*paradise*?

He straightened, a bullish grin still plastered on his face. He walked back to the ashtray, picked up his cigar, and returned to where we sat. "Original stuff. Can't beat it." He puffed the smoke right into Robert's face.

I could hardly restrain myself as my lips pressed tightly. Robert nearly suffocated once when there was a small kitchen fire in his college dorm room. He and smoke didn't mix well. His jaw twitched as he struggled not to show pain.

I sat forward, unable to contain the sight. "Why don't you ask me instead—what I think of your jailhouse cum sweatshop? I might have a better take on it." The words rolled off my tongue with ease as I could barely hide my disgust with the man's behavior. He gripped Robert's chair but didn't move. I saw that Robert was starting to choke, making me more determined to shift the man's attention to me. "C'mon, are you shy or simply weaker than a girl?"

Ah, then he sprung to his feet like lightning and was up in my face in two seconds. At that point, Robert was gasping for precious air, and I rested knowing that, now, he'd be fine.

"You know, I was going to take you last—for several reasons." The man's eyes ran over my body from head to toe, stopping at every curve. I felt as though I'd gotten stripped, yet with my clothes on. "He kept you all to himself all this while. It's time for a change."

Robert coughed then, clearing his lungs. "Now, you leave her alone," he barked.

But the bald man laughed, his jagged teeth none too pleasing to look at. Then he ran a parched finger along my jawline.

I tightened my jaw, folding in my lips as his finger approached them. If I could, I would have slapped his gritty finger off my face.

"Don't you touch her!" Robert shouted from beside me.

Weirdly, that stopped the man, and he rose and walked away. He dropped his spent cigar into an ashtray then picked up a sheet of paper. Then his sheepish grin returned as he read it and looked up at us once more. "I'm going to tell you why you're here. The New Rulebook was developed right here. In this very room. We wanted something we could sell to private corporations, law enforcement agencies, governments, essentially both public and private sector clients—something to appeal to everyone. Then we hit it. The New Rulebook! Through The New Rulebook's groundbreaking, innovative, singular sight, we could restore order and civility to the world." He slid one hand into his pocket arrogantly and gloated.

"When we have The New Rulebook fully operational, criminals will get caught in a fraction of the time. People will be deterred from criminal behavior. Our company, Cortexe Corp., will become a force to be reckoned with. We'll have unlimited access to international surveillance and security grids. Simply put, we will rule the world—"

"With a single click," I cut in, every word dressed in sarcasm.

He nodded then laughed. "There you go, Ruby! I see you're catching on pretty fast." No one else as much as smiled—not even his men who were flanking us. He stared at me like I was a savory meal to be devoured.

"Now that's where you two come in." He stepped right in front of me. "You're a businesswoman. You understand cost and you understand profit. So I'm going to make you an offer." He walked back to his desk, picked up a satellite phone—which looked much like the one the man who'd stopped Robert and me at my apartment building doors had—then he returned. He squatted, all grinning now gone.

I braced for whatever he was about to say or do.

"I'm going to ask you once. If you give me the right answer, I'll let you both walk out of here." He lit another cigar and puffed it in my face. I didn't like it, but I preferred it was my face and not Robert's. "You tell me where the missing ten percent of The New Rulebook software is, and I'll let you both go scot-free. It's that simple."

I gazed at the screen monitoring the employees who were working like ant colonies in their black and white uniforms. I remembered the windows, painted with white metal bars. So I spun to him. "What happens to the investigation for the murder I was framed for?"

Robert jumped forward in his seat. "Ruby, no, please don't do it!"

I nodded to him. "I'm not. Calm down." I faced the man again, waiting for a response.

His grin began to return. "What happens?" He drew in another puff of smoke. "We'll take it one step at a time, Ruby. One step at a time. We can cross that bridge when we get there. For right now, the software is our first priority. Then we'll talk—unless your life and that of your friend isn't worth very much to you."

I sat up straight having had enough of his badgering. "I'll tell you three things. First, you should be ashamed to bargain with an innocent lady for her life, after setting me up for a crime I didn't commit. Second, I can see you are not the one in charge. I want to speak to the person in charge if they're not as cowardly as you are. Third, I don't know what you're talking about. But even if I did and I knew where it was, I'd die before giving it to you. *That* should give you something to smoke on besides cigar. Now, if there's nothing else..." I trailed off and sat back.

He returned to his desk, picked up an expensive-looking sculpted-glass piece, and tossed it against the wall. Its shards scattered loosely around. He pinned his eyes on me, teeth gnashing. "That...was your fault. And it...cost a lot of money." He studied Robert then me again, saying nothing for a long time. "Tell me where it is." He spoke threateningly slower this time.

I stared back at him for an equal while, eyes unflinching. "You know what? You and I are done talking. Free us and let us go."

He got close to my face and slapped me so hard it left my skin tingling. His hand then gripped my throat. So I struggled for air.

By then, Robert was shouting and fighting to get out of his restraints. I also heard thumping sounds, like repeated blows against him, as he was beaten by the men holding him down. My heart broke as Robert tumbled to the floor. The sound of him puking coincided with the man's release of his grip on my throat.

I gasped for air.

"I said where is it?!" he yelled, hands balled into a fist, and ready to attack again.

"Stop!" Robert shouted repeatedly.

"Shut up!" his men were now yelling at Robert.

More chaos followed as I tried to clear my throat to breathe.

"Bring her to me. Walk Towers." A voice calmly came through via overhead speakers, and the authoritative voice reverberated around the room.

Everyone halted, and his men exchanged looks then glanced at their boss.

"Repeat," the bald man replied, looking up toward a speaker planted at the rim of the ceiling.

"I said walk Towers. Now." The voice sounded authoritative enough to avoid any arguments with the order. My guess that the boss had a boss was right. I knew he was too chipper to be in charge, especially for someone who was about to lose his company's greatest technological investment.

Something crossed his face briefly, but I couldn't tell whether that was a good or bad sign. He pivoted to his men, nodding toward Robert. "You heard the man. Go ahead and do as he says."

Two men lifted Robert off the chair, to his feet and began walking him toward the door.

Robert stopped then. "Wait. Please." The men paused briefly as Robert swung around to me. "The place where we'd made macaroni and cheese, it's yours as an early birthday present for your new office. The keys are at, well...you know where I usually keep keys."

I swallowed hard as my throat tightened.

He paused and inhaled deeply, his voice breaking a bit. "I'm still a Christian, Ruby, and I'm still in love with you." His words came soft and tender into my heart this time, despite the pain filling his eyes.

My insides churned with each word he spoke. So much so that I wanted to reach over, hug him, and tell him we could sort this all out. But we couldn't. Not when I was rooted to this chair and unwillingly held down by hands stronger than mine. He turned back to the men without another word, and they led him out, his frame disappearing as the door closed. Then I was left alone with the monster.

As soon as silence settled in the room, he motioned toward his men. "Untie her. I want her to see this."

~

"Y ou see, The New Rulebook is very important to my CEO and me, the COO. I can bargain with you and try to convince you to give it up. But him, he'll *show* you how important."

He cut off my restraints and took me by the hand, walking me toward the window. "By the time this is over, I hope it will demonstrate how far we're ready to go with this." He pressed a button, and the white walls slid back, revealing a window with its white metal bars very visible. He prodded me closer to it and pointed toward the right.

To me, this seemed like the front of the building, but I was not sure. My heart was beating so rapidly, it was threatening to burst out of my chest. Things had progressed so fast that I had to stop my thoughts from spinning. How did Robert and I get into this? First and foremost, why did I call him? I now regretted doing so. I should've just gone to the cops, and he would have been safe right now. Even worse, I didn't know where they took him. Maybe by 'walk' him, they meant to let him go. After all, he had nothing they wanted. But what if I was wrong and their goal was otherwise? I'd had very little time to consider their possible plans when they'd led him out. Moreover, he'd seemed calm enough, like he was ready to face their next plans but had also been scared at the same time. But...how could that be?

Confused and desperate, I looked at the man pleadingly for the first time. "What are you going to do? If it's to Robert, please don't."

He didn't respond. He didn't even acknowledge that I'd said anything.

"There." He pointed out the window at a vehicle coming through the parking lot. I recognized it as the boxlike truck they'd brought us here in. It seemed to be driving rather slowly, inching its way off the Cortexe Corps office grounds. Then the main gate slid shut behind it. Robert must be inside it. Behind the truck, high walls now obscured much of my view as I observed it veering right.

Moments later, a loud boom vibrated outside, interrupting the quietness. I gasped, craning my neck close to the window while scouring the view. A plume of smoke and occasional tongues of flame billowed skyward, trailing the bend—the same corner where I'd seen the vehicle turn. Apprehension swelled inside me for Robert. I clutched a fistful of my hair, unsure what to do with myself. Then, in greater desperation for my lifelong friend, I reached over and grabbed the hand of the COO, searching questioningly into his eyes and hoping by some slim chance he'd say what I just saw wasn't real. His eyes stayed glued to the dark smoke rising to the sky, and him, looking satisfied. I tore my hands away from him like he was a contagion. He shrugged a relaxed shoulder, appearing unconcerned. "Now you see how we walk people out around here."

"Robert! Robert!" I screamed, unable to contain the fire of anguish burning in my belly.

The man calmly stepped back to his desk as though nothing had happened. But my world had been shredded.

The entire room swam in my eyes while my heart shattered as though it was breaking into a million pieces—and was still breaking further. I gasped for air as I grabbed the windows, struggling not to believe my eyes, but the still-rising smoke confirmed my worst fear. Robert was gone. I felt some strong hands restraining me, but I didn't care. Robert's face, which always held a cheer, was permanently imprinted on my soul. His smile that always brightened my day, his voice that meant I was safe—were all gone, poof, because someone wanted to rule the world. Sobbing, I fell to the ground. My voice rose higher until it filled the room with anguished wails. I cried until I had no more tears to shed. Feeling spent, I sat on the ground, holding my aching head in my hands, swaying back and forth. But the fire of anguish still burned within me.

Right about now, Robert would have asked if I wanted an aspirin. Fresh tears brewed and then spilled over onto my cheeks. To be honest, if I'd known what they meant, he would never have left this room. I would have given them what they wanted so they could let us go—or at least let Robert go safely. But I also knew him well enough to know he would've never left me in enemy hands. No. He would rather give himself in exchange for me.

Then it dawned on me that he might have suspected they were going to kill him. Maybe that was the acceptance I'd seen on his face. But why would he do such when he knew what losing him would do to me? I stopped at the thought and asked myself. *Or did he?* I wiped my tears and blinked away those teardrops perching on my lashes as guilt took over.

How could Robert have known what losing him would do to me when I didn't tell him so? After all, when Robert had told me that he was in love with me, all I did was tell him he had bad timing. He told me of his new faith, and I didn't bother asking more. He tried to make me understand, and I pushed him further away. I was the only person he had. If anything, I was the one person who should have understood the news. Or at least, have tried to understand. Now, I'd lost my chance. I couldn't tell him all of what he'd meant to me. I couldn't thank him for the good times we'd shared. I couldn't—wouldn't live—without him. From this moment on, I'd live my life and his. I'd give him a legacy he'd be proud of. He would have wanted me to start right here and to start right now. So, I'd made up my mind. I'd obliterate The New Rulebook. Then I'd bring this entire place down with it.

I rose to full height, appearing somber and calm

outwardly but being far from it inside me. I wiped my tears away. Then I dried my nostrils with the hem of my shirt. I sniffed back to stop my nose from running further. Then I walked over to him. "Take me to the CEO. Now." I coolly requested.

He gave me one look, laughed hard, then patted me on the arm and rubbed his palms together. This time, his actions disgusted me even more thoroughly, but I stayed calm. "Good choice. Now you understand what I meant earlier. I'm glad you chose to cooperate." He ordered his men to open the doors, and they obeyed. The doors glided open in a circular fashion as before. We walked through, with three of his men in tow, who pointed their guns forward and were ready to fire.

7

BLESSED IS THE MAN WHO TRUSTS IN THE LORD, AND whose trust is the Lord. -Jeremiah 17:7

"I'm surprised." Ice rocks stacked upon each other inside an empty wine glass lifted with obvious pride. The CEO's back was turned to me when we entered. Something about his voice sounded oddly familiar, though I couldn't pin it down yet.

"About what?" I maintained my composure. Inside, I still mourned my sudden loss of Robert, but I had to look strong when facing the man who'd taken Robert from me with an evil command. Searing pain tore through the tendons of my heart, leaving nothing but my human shell grasping for a reason why anyone would do what he'd done. With great effort, I focused on the space in front of me so my overwhelming grief didn't bubble outward. I looked around me and saw not a single spot anywhere. The pristine condition of this large room made my skin prick. There was no smell, not even of cleanness. It was just...pristine.

He spun and began approaching me, holding one wine glass in each hand. He was of average height and wore wide sunglasses. They covered his entire upper face, all the way into his hairline, which was strangely dyed white. His solid-white linen suit was just as pristine as this room. A black bracelet cuffing one arm and black shoes contrasted with the suit. He was wearing something like an earpiece, but it was not a regular kind because it was actually scrambling his voice as he spoke, making it come out weird, techno-groovy. But...why would he find it necessary to scramble his voice?

"You didn't do what The New Rulebook predicted." He stopped a few feet away, his shoes shining under the bright lights. Another table—all marble this time—slid out from the wall next to him, with wine bottles set in order within it. He grabbed one bottle and poured it. White wine tumbled from the bottle onto the ice-cube rocks, each glass foaming a little at the top. When he finished, he handed me one glass.

But I declined. "No, thank you."

He withdrew his hand. "You didn't scurry your law-abiding self to the cops to report on the"—he drew in a deep breath—"the murder you witnessed, solely, if I might add." He laughed sarcastically. "For starters, who would even believe such a tale?"

I said nothing but kept my eyes on his every move.

"You were supposed to call those emergency folks, get down to the station, and give your testimony, and when you leave, everything gets interesting while I continue my...business. So you think you achieved anything by calling your little friend and coming over here acting all macho?" His voice rose a pitch higher, but then he took another calming breath. "No. For your information, you didn't. Actually, you just made things easier for me."

A mocking smile marked the corners of his mouth as he came closer. He held his breath briefly as though struggling to control himself. Then he exhaled.

"Let me break tomorrow's headlines to you a little early. In the morning, the press will report that you, Ruby Masters, killed a Cortexe Corp. employee, whom you were supposed to make a delivery for, in an attempt to rob her. You ran away, and your friend here, Robert—oh, I'm sorry you lost him..." A fake smile plastered on his face. "You know, sacrifices are sometimes necessary."

By then, I was panting, and my hands were curved into balled fists. How dare he mention Robert in such a manner!

He continued, "Then you proceeded to kill your friend, Detective—no, Sergeant—Sergeant Towers, when he found out you were a murderer. That makes him a hero and you a criminal. He gets a star; you get cuffs and go away for a long time. Case closed."

He took a sip of wine at the end of his evil narration. "Now, I can keep you here as long as necessary until I get what I need from you. Then, when I'm good and ready, I'll toss you to the police dogs to sniff you out. Or you can give me what I want—what Violet gave you—the missing ten percent of *my* New Rulebook, with which I'll change the world, and maybe we can tweak the news tomorrow so you don't end up on death row." He pompously shoved one hand into his pocket. "Of course, the choice is up to you. You have six hours from now."

He then poured more wine into his glass. "You and your friend evaded me for too long. Dragging me all over town chasing you. Now he's gone. And I'm not going to chase you around or play games with you, all right?" He stared at me through his sunglasses. I could feel his eyes on me even though I couldn't see them.

"That's the first—and last—time it will ever happen."

I stared back with an unflinching gaze. "You mean the murder part? Because that would be a nice break the world will surely appreciate from you."

He straightened like my words had struck a nerve, rubbing his palms together—a trait I guessed he shared with his COO. "We still lack ten-percent content, but we're at ninety-nine-point-nine-percent accurate prediction levels. Isn't that fantastic? The New Rulebook—that's how the game is now played— for the whole world in a few hours." His jagged laughter bristled my ears as he moved away.

Then I couldn't resist spilling my next words to puncture his pride. "You forgot about your point-one percent chance of utter failure? In fact, I would be worried about that if I were you."

He swung around so fast that some wine spilled onto the immaculate floors. He randomly looked daggers at one of his men.

The unfortunate man—with a weather-beaten face and rough skin—scurried to the desk and grabbed a handful of napkins.

Then the CEO faced me again, rising anger sparkling in his face. He brought his face inches from mine as his alcohol-dense breath poured down my lungs with an overwhelming burst.

He pointed a finger at me. "The only person who needs to be worried in this room is you." His crude and unnatural sounding voice remained chilly with calculated calm. He straightened, but again with a finger, he beckoned the man with the weather-beaten face closer. "Take her."

The henchman approached, eyes set on me, flexing his arms in preparation for any aggression from me. But aggression was far from my plans. It was worthless resisting them—at least physically.

The immaculate man—as I'd decided to name him—smiled when I was led away while he gulped down the remaining contents of his glass.

~

With me now locked up, men's lively conversation outside drifted beneath the doorway, into the room where I lay. Window blinds were slightly parted, filtering in natural light. The curtains were all solid gray, and the room smelled a bit musky. A small sink sat at the rightmost corner of the room. Judging from the size, I hadn't expected such normal accommodations while held in captivity at the headquarters of Cortexe Corp. —nevertheless, I kept my focus on how to escape.

Deep underground jail cells filled with people whom The New Rulebook identified as having "probability greater than 90 percent of deviation" were what I thought I would have seen here. But I was wrong. Unless these unusual but basic accommodations were for people like me—people they desperately wanted something from and were willing to play nice to get it. I had no doubt they'd do away with me soon as they got what they wanted—just like they did with Robert. Tears welled up my eyes, but I shoved them down. This wasn't the time to cry. This was the time to use my sorrow as fuel.

I turned over to the other part of the room. It had been about two hours since the men had put me in here, three hours tops. I didn't have a watch so I wasn't exactly sure. Within minutes, they'd set up alarms all around the room, and then left two guards at the door, one stayed with me inside and one outside. The lady guard stationed inside the room shot me a warning, don't-try-anything look. But I smiled to her in a dissuading manner. "Don't worry. If I was going to fight anyone, it's not with you. I would've started with the guys before they got me in here. So relax, okay?"

She said nothing, but her shoulders drooped, proving my words had met their intended mark.

I sat on the edge of the bed, cautious not to trigger the laser beams lined around the bed's perimeter— also separating me from the rest of humanity. A cursory glance told me she was maybe in her twenties, same as I. "What's your name?"

She looked up at me after pausing her fingers tapping away on a piece of tech. She frowned, eyes narrowing as if I'd interrupted something urgent. Then blinking, she returned her focus to her phone-like device.

I sighed at her silent treatment. "You know, if you and I are going to be stuck in here for a while, we might as well start talking." She didn't look up this time, clearly now intent on ignoring me, so I kept on talking, "Do you know who you work for? What they do? Who they are?"

Her hands typed faster.

"Or why and how they hired you?"

Her fingers stopped for a moment—only a moment—before they continued tapping away on her device.

A small laugh escaped my throat, as I no longer cared whether she said anything or not. "Or maybe they just happened to get the right percentage on you, just like me. Perfect fit for setup according to The New Rulebook." I kept on laughing, unable to stop now.

The absurdity of the entire situation, my loss of Robert, the inevitability of what could happen to me, and my present resignation all turned into a teary and hurtful, full-throated laugh session. Afterward, I took a deep, calming breath, and it helped some tension ebb away from my mind. If an opportunity for an escape came, which I highly doubted, I did need to keep my wits about me. She was still typing away like the flapping wings of a butterfly, though appearing more relaxed now.

I turned philosophical. "You know, lady, when they misjudge people like you and me—seemingly defenseless folks used as perfect targets—they make their biggest mistakes. We're not robots that can be manipulated or predicted by a software. Neither are we weak or dispensable as garbage. The human will is a gift from God, and no one can—or should—ever take it away." I glanced at her fingers, now furiously slamming the keys. So I wondered when would either her fingers or the gadget pack up? Also, how come I was beginning to think more about God now? Nevertheless, I let my mouth finish its job.

"You can quit no matter how much they're paying you. Get a new job, at a good place. At least, a company where their goal isn't global destruction. Then you can start a new life. You can start over." More emotionally exhausted than physically, I sighed. Sleep began to overpower my eyelids so I gave in. I turned on my side as I slipped into another realm of existence.

❧

"Hey. Hey, wake up," a hushed female voice interrupted a dream I was having. "Hey! We don't have much time to talk! Wake up."

The voice grew a bit louder, and I remembered where I was. Then I startled awake from sleep. My eyes searched the dim room, and light flashed by the corner near the door. I saw who was waking me up—the lady guard. The one who wouldn't speak to me earlier.

"You said I can start over. Did you mean it, or are you just trying to find a way out of here?"

My eyes were still adjusting, considering the pitch darkness out the window. I wiped a hand over my face and blinked away the remaining drowsiness. "Yes. Yes, I meant what I said. You can start over." I was cautious with my words to ensure I wasn't getting setup—yet again. I flipped the switch on a lightbulb dangling from the ceiling directly above, hanging loosely over the center of the bed.

She jumped up. "Turn off the lights! Now!"

But I'd already seen what was in her hand.

Silence filled the room for over a minute.

Moments later, she spoke again. "I started here as an intern."

I let her take her time to continue.

"I was placed in the Innovation Unit on the top floor with a great view. We used customized IDs to enter the unit—which made us feel special. I was running errands, getting coffee, photocopying, and dreaming of a good recommendation to colleges from Mr. Zendel, if I was ever lucky to meet him—and that was my typical daily routine for three months. Mr. Zendel was a myth to the interns. All of us had heard of him. Large life-sized posters of his image hung everywhere in Cortexe Corp., but no one among us had ever met him in person. That was my goal—to meet him and get a recommendation into college. I thought that if that happened, then I'd definitely make it in." She clicked a small light on, and it reflected off her oval-shaped face, highlighting full lips.

I sat up straight, listening.

She continued, "One day near the end of my internship, I was asked to do a mail run from the ground floor. I'd seen another intern do it every day for months, so I figured it was no big deal. I made my way to the ground floor, taking the stairs as I like to do. When I got to the second floor, I ran into a lady— with an average height and sharp brown eyes—and in my hurry, I mistakenly knocked her leather-bound journal to the ground. A stack of papers flew off, held together by an—"

I gasped. "An eagle-winged clip!"

She sat up across the room. "Yes! How do you know?"

I waved an impatient hand, though doubtful she saw my gesture due to the poor lighting. "Don't worry about that yet, just continue. I'm listening."

She flicked off the light, and we sat in darkness for a

while. "I was in shock. Not because of what she looked like, but *who* she looked like—she was a carbon copy of Mr. Zendel in female form. Speechless, I wondered why we'd never seen her. Then she smiled disarmingly and asked me for a favor. 'Can you drop this into the glove box of the white car parked in the front row at the entrance, please? The driver's door is open.'

"So I introduced myself to her, got her business card, and agreed to help. I was excited even though I thought she was probably in a hurry. I also thought doing this for her would get me closer to my goal of meeting Mr. Zendel in person—and ultimately to getting the college recommendation I badly wanted from him." She laughed sarcastically. "Boy, was I wrong."

I readjusted, leaning on my elbow and holding up my head with my right hand.

"I took the requested detour and dropped off the journal at her car—a posh, flashy ride at that. Then I entered the building and picked up the mail as I was originally sent to do."

She let out a deep breath, but I held mine.

"Back at the Innovation Unit, I did my job as I normally would the rest of the day. Signing off at five o'clock, I headed to my room located on company grounds, without giving a second thought to what happened." She turned the small light back on, crossed her legs on the floor, and rested her head on the wall.

"Early in the morning," her voice now sounded a

little weak, "maybe around four o'clock, heavily armed men burst into my room, ordered my roommate out, and then locked the door behind them. But not before someone else entered, dressed in white suit and pants, hair glistening. Your guess is as good as mine—Mr. Zendel."

I chuckled. "Mr. Immaculate himself." No wonder the voice had sounded vaguely familiar. He was Violet Zendel's twin.

She nodded. "Definitely not the kind of meeting I'd dreamed of having with him—both in terms of the time and place." She coughed, rose, and walked over to the window, peering through the parted blinds. The cover of night stared back at us. "That night, all my dreams came crashing. He accused me of being in collusion with his sister, asking me how long I'd been working with her. I denied all of his accusations flat out, but of course, he didn't believe me. I was roughly cuffed, then transported back to the Cortexe Corp. main complex in the middle of the night, which looked like a ghost town. Heavily armed security guards, who weren't there during the day, shut the gates behind us. I was taken to a twelfth floor, marked X, I didn't know existed. Apparently, someone else had a better view than those of us in the Innovation Unit.

"But the twelfth floor looked very different. There were no windows, at least, none I could see, pristine floors, and people dressed in uniform working desperately—a clock set on the wall for them with a deadline. It was counting down fourteen days. Today is the fourteenth day.

"When I arrived, Ms. Zendel, his sister—"

"Violet," I cut in. "Her name's Violet."

She nodded. "Right, Violet was already seated in a chair by the left side, near a door marked with a caution symbol. He asked them to stand her up when we entered. Then he ordered everyone in black and white uniform out. His men placed me at the opposite side of the room. He stood in the middle and said whichever one of us would choose to give the other person away, got to live. We both remained silent."

She walked over to the corner where she'd sat on the ground earlier, grabbed a water bottle, and sipped, putting it back down. She stood, appearing somewhat eager to finish her story.

"He then came to me and asked what I was sent to do at his sister's car. I thought of what to say that would not implicate me further than I already was. Then I had the right answer. 'She said her car door was open,' I replied, eyes looking straight ahead. He came up and looked into my eyes. I felt as though cold steel was rummaging through my soul, but I didn't flinch. 'Are you saying she sent you all the way downstairs *just* to lock her car for her? You want me to believe that?' he asked, clearly furious. I was shaking inside, and it was truly a matter of time before it showed outwardly. 'I'm an intern, sir. What else would she send me to do?' I pressed.

"Suddenly, she stepped toward him. The guards came in between them, held up their weapons, and seemed ready to attack her. He waved them down and beckoned to her with a finger to speak. 'Let the kid go. She did nothing wrong,' she pleaded for me. But he didn't move. 'What made you believe you could stop me, Violet? You should have known better,' he challenged. She gazed steadily at him but held her ground. I admired her courage.

"'This is not what our parents wanted for this company. You know what you're doing is wrong. Please stop before it's too late. A lot of lives will be affected, Pete. Please listen to me. I'm your sister, your twin. I can't lie to you; you know what I'm telling you is true. You've seen the facts. Why don't you listen?' she pushed, but it seemed like she was pouring more fuel into a blazing fire.

"He didn't yell, though I wished he did. He didn't even shout. He just said, 'You know what to do with her.' So his men scurried to obey. There and then, I saw their resemblance didn't go beyond their faces. He was cold and evil to the core. His sister was very different. She wore a small necklace looped with a tiny cross pendant. She carried herself with grace, despite the choice she just made. She'd chosen to save my life instead of hers.

"I'll never forget how she smiled warmly at me when she was being led out. At the door, she turned and said to me, 'You're very brave. Thank you.' Her brother smiled at her with dead cold eyes as his men led her past him into the elevator doors. 'Goodbye, twin sis.' He shook his head. The corners of his mouth turned downward spitefully, he added, 'All that talent, wasted.' And that was the last I saw of her."

She went to the door, got down on hands and knees on the floor as she peeped underneath. "The guard will return in a few minutes from his break so we have maybe five more minutes." She raised her head to me. "Now you can turn on the lights."

"What about your flashlight?"

She pointed it forward, shaking her head. "Oh no, this is no flashlight. This device neutralizes voice vibrations, sending them out as static on electronic monitoring devices."

"You mean no one knows we're talking?"

She rose. "No. Not at all." She peeped under the door again, readying the stun gun I'd seen in her hand earlier. "Be ready."

I frowned. "Ready for what?"

"You'll see."

8

FOR WHO IS GOD BUT THE LORD? AND WHO IS A ROCK except our God... -Psalm 18:31

R OBERT

Burning coughs sputtered through my lungs, and I spat out dark-colored spittle, thankful when I saw there was no blood in it. I lay on my back, allowing several rounds of cough spasms wracking my body to die down. I raised myself on my knees and looked above the rim of the gutter. Smoke fumes still blew skyward from the explosion. It made me so glad that I'd purchased rapid-explosion protection for my bulletproof vest! I remembered it had cost me a month's paycheck but was so thankful that it literally just saved my life. It went into action the moment the explosion occurred as the hoodie shot upward, covering my face, and the leg shields spread down the sides of my legs. I'd then covered my face with both arms, sustaining only minor injury. But the guy next to me wasn't so lucky. I'd covered him to offer some protection. Both guards seated in front of us in the driver's two-row section were killed instantly. I guessed that they were equally ambushed with their boss' plan.

"Hey, hey. Wake up." I slapped the detective's cheeks, hoping he would revive soon. "Detective, c'mon. We haven't got much time." More coughs rattled me, and I bent over to get them out. When I rose again, I was so glad to hear him sneeze. "Now, that's what I'm talking about. Take it slow and easy. You'll get your breath back." I held him up a little and winced. His arms were partly burned by the explosion. I wasn't sure about the rest of him that I couldn't see. I peered into his face. "What's your name?"

He looked at me, blinked, and yelled, "What happened? Am I dead? I'm feeling a lot of pain." His voice kept rising so I needed to quiet him down.

"Listen, buddy. No, you're not dead. We were in an explosion together. We're at Cortexe Corp. headquarters. Do you remember?"

His eyes roamed aimlessly for a moment. Then they brightened. "Yes! Those..." He released a string of cuss words that made me cringe.

"Okay, take it easy. Calm down. No need to cuss,

all right? Tell me your name, and what you were here for."

He squinted at me, his eyes narrowing. "Why all these questions? My arms hurt!"

Considering our circumstance, my patience was wearing thin. "Listen, I'm a police officer with the MPD, and I was abducted and brought here with a friend. They think I'm dead and possibly think we're both dead right now. I overheard them say you were a detective when they put you in the truck with me. So now are you going to tell me who you are?" Threatening to leave him could make it go faster, but I chose not to. It was not necessary. Moreover, I would never leave anyone, officer or civilian, behind.

He gripped my torn shirt, ripping it further. "Listen to me. My name is Detective Mike Argan. I'm in the Special Investigative Division of the MPD."

I frowned. "I've never heard of that division before."

"We're undercover. We report to the captain directly. Our personnel files are kept under lock and key." He paused and flinched. "I feel like I'm still on fire. Help me sit up."

I obliged and lifted him up to a sitting position. "So what was your mission here?"

He winced and then grunted in pain. "Our unit was investigating something called The New Rulebook, supposed to go operational sometime today."

My heartbeat quickened. "Wow. That's the reason my friend, Ruby, and I are here. The New Rulebook is why we were abducted. Except they framed her for murder yesterday, so she's on the run."

He nodded toward the complex. "We have an inside source, Violet Zendel, twin sister to the CEO."

I sighed while wondering whether I should tell him or not?

"She's the one I came to see today."

I frowned as I realized I couldn't keep the news about Violet's demise hidden from him. "That's why you were scheduled for murder. Violet is dead. She was killed yesterday, and my friend was framed for her murder. Then they captured us and led us here, to this complex."

His shoulders drooped as his face turned glum. "I was sanctioned off the grid for the past forty-eight hours, so I was at a rural location. As a result, I had no access to technology of any kind except my secure phone. All in preparation for today. I worked on this lead for months, and I can't believe how this turned out. At the beginning, when Violet began to cooperate with law enforcement, she said she feared for her life, like she was being watched. I offered to place her in protective custody. But she'd refused and said that no one could protect her from her brother—or from The New Rulebook. She was getting ready to resign and go away quietly, so as not to betray her brother nor be part of what he was doing. I still can't believe she's dead." He shook his head. "You have to be heartless to kill your own blood."

His chest rose and fell faster, and I suspected his blood pressure was probably increasing too. "Listen, you need to calm down, or you might not make it. We have no backup and no one's coming, so you have to stay conscious for a while. I'm going to need your help to stop this ring. My friend is still in there, and I have to go get her out. But you can only help me if you control your pulse. Can you do that for me?"

Pain glinted through his eyes, but he endured. "Yes. Yes, I can. For Violet's sake." More tears shone through his gaze, so I knew.

I realized why he hurt so much because I saw the same pain in me now. His pain wasn't only physical—it was also emotional. "You loved her."

More tears welled up in his eyes, confirming my suspicion. "Yes, and I'll do whatever I can to stop them. I won't let them destroy more innocent lives."

I thought to ask again about her, but I held back. "I'll see when we have an opening, and then I'll come back for you, okay?"

He nodded, barely but visibly. "You go ahead. I'll be right here. I'm fine."

But even as he said it, I was afraid for him. I bound his wounds the best I could, but I had to leave some open when I ran out of clothing. I was left with the pants on my waist; everything else I'd already used for first aid. I placed him by a patch of bushes, hiding him behind sufficient tall grasses, and covered him up to his neck. Crawling on all fours, I climbed into the gutter, stomping on some dirt and wastewater. I rolled up my pant legs for dryness and took my shoes in one hand. I walked for a while before approaching the gate to peer through a crack on the edge, but it was too high to jump over it. Frustrated, I found nothing else leading inside.

I looked around me. Then I stopped and smiled. Nothing else fit for entry—except the gutter—which was wide enough and ran right into the complex. That was my way in.

I got sufficiently close to the main gate then slid underneath the five-inch-thick gates through the gutter into the complex. I was glad this part of the gutter was not as wet as I'd thought it would be and had no pungent smell. Soon, I was in. The main building stood about forty feet away from me. Men guarded the gate, chatting away like grasshoppers. But I lowered myself, slipping past the guards.

I reached a curve where the gutter led from the main building. I figured I'd have to come out here above ground in order to reach my destination. But I couldn't do that while it was still daylight. I needed to wait for the sun to set. Where I was now was too exposed, so I risked getting caught. Left with no other options, I made the tough choice to go back out. I squeezed my body to flip around inside the gutter. I felt as though I might have broken something, but right now, I didn't care. Getting Ruby out of there was my priority since I knew who'd framed her for murder. I'd arrest them at the right time, but first, I needed to save Ruby.

I swallowed at the thought of her and imagined what she must be going through, knowing she probably thought I was dead. It hurt to imagine what the man could do to her.... And my fingers balled into a fist. But I cautioned myself to stay calm, so I inhaled. *Focus. Get to her first.*

I glanced behind me, now outside the complex again. With my dwindling options, I knew the detective out there could be my only help with information, so I turned around and headed back toward him.

When I reached him, I asked the man a few more questions to aid me in rescuing Ruby. "Tell me everything you know about The New Rulebook, including everything you witnessed." He struggled to rise, so I propped his head up with my left arm. The setting sun cast a shadow in the distance, bringing out the contrasting beauty of nature, compared to the steely-cold concrete complex standing against its light.

His eyes were red and puffy, and it looked like he began crying as soon as I left so I was glad I returned. I rubbed the pain aching my back as I pushed further. "Detective, I need to know everything that could help me save Ruby. Please, anything at all can help."

He blinked a couple of times then swallowed before he spoke. "What I'm about to tell you is all I know. Six months ago, the police found a body near a high-rise downtown. I was on tour with criminal investigations at the time and was assigned to the investigation team for the case. Nothing stood out at first, as it seemed like a routine crime scene." He coughed, and I repositioned him to lean on his side.

"One thing didn't fit, though. Some officers said it was a close-range shot, but the blood-spatter pattern seemed otherwise to me and my partner. The trajectory of the bullet shown by the entry wound on the victim indicated a sniper had shot him from a well-calculated angle. My partner and I sent our conflicting observation to the senior agent-in-charge. When the report was released, it said the incident was a cold case, no leads. That the victim was shot at a close range. But we knew that wasn't true. So my partner called the office to register our disapproval of the report. He was killed by a hit and run on his way back from lunch the next day."

I frowned in shock, but something was unclear to me. "Don't get me wrong, but why would they kill him and leave you?"

He shook his head like he was going through the pain all over again. "Because he signed the report."

I pressed my lips tightly as this thing kept getting grimmer. They'd killed the detective's partner, just as they killed Violet and left Ruby to take the blame. When would this whole thing stop?

The detective continued, "Everyone involved in the investigation was reassigned. That was when I knew something was up. However, I had to stick to their version. I figured if I tried to investigate it, then it could turn the other cops against me. I can't afford that kind of fight. I don't need it either."

By now, the sun had almost fully disappeared.

"I need to get onto my other side," the detective said. "This side now hurts."

So I raised him up while carefully helping him turn to his side.

"I didn't know who to trust. A couple of weeks ago, my captain called me into his office and told me they were putting together a high-stakes Special Investigations Unit to investigate that unsolved murder. We were to report to him and him alone. He said there could be a bad apple among us, but he intended to flush them out, his words not mine. I was to coordinate the team. Having lost my partner questionably, he felt I'd be more motivated to get to the bottom of things. And he was right."

"Do you have any leads on who killed the victim?"

He shook his head. "We hit a wall every time we asked questions. We dug deep, but we kept coming back empty. Until one afternoon, when I got a phone call from the coroner. He asked me to come over to the morgue immediately—alone—so I did."

The sky began to seem darker than just nightfall. Since it was springtime and April when sometimes it got cloudy, I didn't let it bother me. I turned my attention back to the detective.

"I got to the morgue, and he led me into the cremation room. He said he'd examined the body when the case was still active, but unknown to him, he'd missed something. We walked over to the body, and he raised the sheets. He then proceeded to raise one arm, walked over, and raised the other arm. He asked me what I saw. I said they were armpits. But he asked me to look closer with a magnifying glass. Then I saw a tattoo, actually two tattoos, one on each armpit, obscured by all the hair the man had. That was why it hadn't been visible until they shaved him. But they didn't see it at the time because no one thought anything would be in the armpits. When I

observed closer, I saw the tattoo on one armpit read
The Rulebook. And the other one had Cortexe Corp.
imprinted on it. I asked them to hold off on the
cremation."

My ears tingled at the words I heard and almost
sounded unbelievable. But I knew he told the truth,
considering everything he said was corroborating
what Ruby and I had experienced from the Cortexe
Corp. leadership so far. Someone had been killed over
this Rulebook before? I shuddered. It was probably
how Violet Zendel knew she would get killed before it
actually happened. She might have known the dead
guy, or maybe, even worked with him.

"Cortexe Corp.?"

He nodded slightly. "Cortexe Corp. I went ahead
and checked out their website. According to the offi-
cial site, they're located in virtual space. No physical
address was listed. They deal in the latest technological installations for individuals, offices, and companies. They install computers, surveillance equipment,
home security systems and more. Aside from that,
their website was void of any real contact information.
I got especially concerned when I read that they
partner with major home protection companies on
nationwide grids. Meaning, they have access to most
homes, offices, and companies by extension. I
wondered what they could do with such widespread
surveillance access. Then I realized that maybe our
victim was not an accident at all."

Some wind gusted by, and I shielded my eyes from
the dust. He was speaking slower now and taking

more breaths in-between. I knew I'd soon start heading back, but I wanted to hear everything he had to say first.

"I took my suspicions and new facts to the captain. As a result, he added The Rulebook to our investigation, asking us to get to the bottom of whatever it was. He said that, if it was important enough for the victim to hide it, maybe it was important enough for us to know about it. I searched the internet and virtually everywhere, yet I found nothing about any rulebook —unless it was for toy games. It was frustrating, so I decided to go about it the other way around. I went back to the drawing board and started searching for more information about Cortexe Corp."

He coughed again. "I found only one contact phone number listed for a Cortexe Corp. Learn For A Day Conference. I called the number and registered. I was asked for a school registration confirmation, which the captain helped me secure from a local college. I sent it to them before being approved to attend. I was provided the address to this location via an encrypted message. That was the first time I came here. When I arrived, I couldn't believe my eyes. Young people, mostly in their late teens and early twenties, were all here. In fact, I looked like a grandpa among them. If Violet was still alive, maybe—"

Tears glistened in his eyes as his voice choked. I patted him lightly on the shoulder to help ease his pain of loss. By this time, it was getting so dark that I could barely see my hand anymore.

"A test was administered after we arrived, soon

after that they separated us into two groups. One group stayed for the rest of the conference, the other was taken to a part of the building that looked like a cube with black dots on its exterior. I couldn't tell what it was or what they were doing inside there. When we came down to leave, they all had small, sealed packets, but we didn't. Also, their faces bore huge smiles. I tried to sneak upstairs while the conference was going on, but a security officer intercepted me and reported me to Violet."

Color seemed to be returning to his cheeks. That was a good sign.

"Was that the first time you two met?"

"Yes. After the security guy stepped outside, she asked me if I was a cop. Something in her eyes made me know I may have met an ally. I said yes. She gave me her contact information and said never to show up uninvited at the complex again or I'd end up dead."

"Have you been back here since?"

He shook his head. "No. Not until today. I guess she was right, as they tried killing me today. But Violet had been so helpful to me. We literally talked for ten minutes every day. She was warm and kind, but sharp-witted as ever. It wasn't surprising that I fell in love with her. On the other hand, she cooperated fully with our investigation, providing me with as much information as she could and asking me to help her in stopping The New Rulebook's launch."

"Did she tell you when that was supposed to happen?"

"Yes. She said it was today. She also said that she'd

be ready to go after we stopped it together. I promised her the police would get her out the moment she asked, if things went south before now, except she didn't get the chance to leave on her own." A frown creased his brow.

"Why not try to stop it ahead of time before it launches?"

He let out a scowl. "That was because the time for the launch couldn't be reset. There was only one person who could do that, and that was the person who built it. It would have taken months, and Violet couldn't do it without getting caught. Moreover, that wasn't what her brother wanted—for it to move forward—so it wouldn't happen without significant risk to her."

"Who officially owns the company?"

"Though their parents started the company from humble beginnings, they handed it off to Pete and Violet when they both got sick, making Pete the CEO, being a man. Then he went off with his own agenda. She said she would have left, but after she realized his intentions weren't just surveillance for law enforcement, but rather psychopathic, she had to build something that could stop The New Rulebook and stop him. She added that the only person who could do it in her stead was already dead."

I looked up at the darkened sky and could sense the opportunity for reentry slipping. "I'm assuming she meant the murder victim you had identified in town."

He nodded in confirmation. "Yes, she said he was

an analyst heading up the project before her. He apparently disagreed with her brother, and her brother must've had him killed. Then she took over the project, starting from scratch. She didn't think he would hurt her even if he later found out that she'd helped us. I guess she was wrong about him and was wrong from the start about what he was capable of. He's a monster. The things she told me he had done were things that I could never believe any human being was capable of doing...so evil—except now, I've experienced it from him firsthand. He'd ordered his men to 'walk me.' Now I know what that means." His shoulders trembled as he coughed. Then it subsided again.

This time, his voice came through clearer. If he kept talking, I was hopeful he might make it until help arrived. "Hang in there, buddy. I'll be going back inside the complex soon. Somehow, I'll get us help out of here."

He gave me a weak smile. "There are too many similarities to ignore. Too many facts add up on their own even without further digging."

No doubt about that. I shifted my crouch, my feet tingling from growing numb. "Violet and her predecessor ended up dead, a Rulebook and a New Rulebook were developed—"

"Two victims were killed at high-rise buildings," he took over. "By snipers camouflaged as close-range shooters, this time framing an innocent witness as a murderer, and attempted the murder of two cops—

their rap sheet is going to be long—very long, my friend."

I was calm as I remembered Ruby and prayed she wouldn't be next on their kill list. "They pinned the murder on my friend, Ruby, so cops like us don't start linking the dots and succeed in stopping them." My mind was made up, and I didn't want her to die out here. I couldn't—and wouldn't—let it happen.

~

I t takes nearly losing someone to recognize their true worth, I once heard. That rang true for me right now. I could still see her face when they "walked" me out of that room hours ago. Though now, it felt like that was a lifetime ago. For eighteen years, we'd been a part of each other's lives. We ate together, fought together, and laughed together. Today, we got torn apart by forceful hands. Right. *Just when I fall in love with her.* Feeling frustrated, I ran a hand through my hair.

Ruby. I could almost see her face, sense her smile, and feel the kindness even in her jokes. How long had I thought about her, smiled when I remembered something funny she'd said in the past? Now I knew I must've loved her from the moment I saw her. I just didn't know it then.

At this point, the sun had completely set as I looked far away in the distance, ready to make my second trip back into the Cortexe Corp. complex. But my thoughts wandered to Ruby again.

Red. I gave her that nickname. We'd been friends for a few weeks when I nicknamed her Red. But somehow, it felt easier on my tongue than her real name, though I liked it too. After all, everyone knew rubies were red. Even now, I felt a smile tug at the corners of my mouth. Though she'd asked me to call her Ruby instead of Red yesterday, I knew it was born out of anger or fear of what could happen if things changed between us relationship-wise.

Sometimes, I felt as though I knew her so well that I understood her more than myself. It amazed me how we'd clicked from the day a boy tried to get at her at the orphanage. Initially, I'd observed the quarrel from a distance before I got involved. To this day, I couldn't tell why I fought for her that first time. The second time was a much clearer choice. The lightbulb at the hallway was out so neither of them had seen me approach them. I heard when the bully had threatened her. So I watched her reaction. For a six-year-old, I was stunned by her graceful and fearless stance though faced with an obvious disadvantage. She stood like she could take on the world with her little finger and not even bat an eyelid.

I was blown away. I knew I had to step in. I had to stand up for her. I wanted her friendship, and I wanted her to be a part of my life. Since then, we grew up helping each other through tough situations. Like when Ruby's aunt—her only known relative—who visited her once every couple of months, lost her battle with cancer. We were twelve, but I saw how much Ruby suffered emotionally when she'd received the news. Through the years, we were a staple in one another's lives. We were just two people who understood each other well and fiercely defended and liked each other.

Red usually stood up for me whenever anyone came at me, without any hesitation. I could see she cared about me just as I did about her. But I didn't think she ever saw us being more than friends. Going forward, if she decided that was how things would continue to be, it could be tough for me, but I'd choose to respect it.

"Okay, man, I've got to go back in." I patted Mike on the shoulder. Then I gave him my watch. "Here. Have this. So you can keep track of time." I needed to know the time inside too, but for now, leaving my watch with him only meant that I'd have to work faster without it.

He grabbed my arm as I attempted to leave. "Be careful. If you can't stop them, at least save your friend." He looked progressively weaker, especially within the past hour. Earlier, I'd chosen to stay with him a little longer to monitor his condition, so I was asking him about his favorite sports teams to pass time. Now, however, I silently prayed he'd be able to hang on until any help arrived. Prayer had been such a new and rewarding experience for me. Since I received Jesus, new experiences had trailed my understanding of how life worked and was meant to work. I was trying to share my experiences with Ruby, but she'd shut me out. Now, I uttered a desperate prayer on her behalf, "God, You shut the mouths of lions for

Daniel. Please keep Ruby safe and alive in Jesus' name. I cannot imagine my life without her." I knew that the pain alone could kill me faster than the explosion ever could. I rose and made my way toward the gutter, reentering Cortexe Corp.—for the last time.

9

"...But with the temptation, [God] will provide the way of escape..." –
1 Corinthians 10:13

Rough edges scraped my arms as I squeezed through the gutter again. Inside, the complex floodlights surrounded the main building like swarms. My hands gripped the side of the gutter as I raised my head, peeping over the edge. People clad in suits milled around, holding sheets of paper and folders. A few alighted from posh cars and stepped right into the front foyer of the main complex. Significant foot traffic at this time of the night in an office complex was unusual, so that alerted me. If what Detective Mike had said was true, then the launch of The New Rulebook was the reason for these people's presence. Two guards approached, so I ducked and waited for a few moments before raising my head again. As I looked again, to my relief, they were now some distance away.

I crawled over to the diversion point where I'd reached earlier on my first go. I stopped to look around again. Then I kicked my feet up in the air involuntarily as a rodent climbed on my toes. The huge rat shrieked in terror, attracting a guard's attention. He turned around and started walking toward where I was.

"What's up, man?" the second guard asked, still standing afar off.

"Wait. I think I heard something." The first guard's voice now sounded close—much too close. Flashlight reflections against the wall swirled near my face, so I collapsed flat into the gutter while silently praying that I wouldn't be found out.

"Where did you hear it coming from?" the second guard asked, some impatience lacing his voice.

"Around here."

The second guard approached, too, flashing his lights. "Hey, I don't see anything here. Come on, we've got to go. The launch is starting soon." By now, they'd reached the very edge of the gutter, and I held my breath. Slowly, their footsteps receded and sounded farther away. "Hey, it could be that those ears of yours need some dewaxing since you're now hearing stuff!" the second guard teased.

I heaved a sigh as I regained my squatting posture,

waiting till they were fully clear before raising my head again.

Everyone who was entering Cortexe Corp. right now had some eagerness visible in their steps. Moments later, water dropped on my arm. Then another drop followed, and yet another. I could hardly believe it chose to rain right now. Within minutes, it became a downpour.

I was soaked and shivering cold. I wondered about Detective Mike's condition outside the gate, but I needed to hurry up for his sake. Due to the rain, my time window had just gotten smaller. Then I remembered something Ruby had said about The New Rulebook. She'd mentioned that vapor clouded their monitoring ability, so I smiled at what could only have been divine timing of this rainfall, to cloak my arrival. "Thank you, Jesus, for the rain of spring." I'd just received my pass into Cortexe Corp.!

I rose from the gutter and ran on the paved surface, letting the rain wash the mess off my feet. I cautiously approached, joining the foot traffic—more like running traffic, since everyone was now desperate to get out of the rain—right into the main Cortexe Corp. complex.

At the door, a few people cast smiling glances at my shirtless chest but most were just rushing through, sorting their drenched attires. Wealthy-looking guests tossed umbrellas onto the floor in anger. Security guards darted back and forth drying the floors, welcoming arrivals, and grabbing umbrellas and wet jackets, then apologizing for the rain conditions, which they had no control over.

I picked up an umbrella to disguise myself, but I was a little too late. I'd been spotted.

A security guard approached me. "Hey."

I stopped in my tracks, and my heart beat faster.

He stood inches away while studying me. With a hand, he beckoned me closer.

My mouth felt dry, although my lips were wet from the rain. My fingers clammed up as I thought of options but found none that didn't lead to me being tossed right back out into the rain—that is, if I was lucky.

"Are you the dancer for the night?"

I hesitated, taking in his words, but making no sense of them. I had only one risk-free answer—a slow nod.

In response, a wide grin covered his face. "Then come on in. Don't be a stranger. Big night for you, huh?" He playfully punched me hard on the arm, and I managed not to wince.

"You have no idea."

"So, what do they have you dancing tonight? Jazz or Blues...oh, now that's something!" He led me into the elevator filled with visitors, who seemed too enthusiastic to notice the stunned expression I'm sure I wore.

As we entered, the uniformed men inside the black-dotted section of the building were working with frenzy. Everyone here seemed dressed to kill—

both figuratively and practically. Guards who were clad in black surrounded the room, and their weapons were pointed down and ready. As I glanced around the room, most of the seated guests were middle-aged men. The youngsters among them were frantically working on computers. The timer on the wall said there were fifteen minutes to go. The excitement in the room was as palpable as my own steadily growing apprehension.

That left me wondering, what happened to Ruby? Where was she? If she was still alive, she would be trying hard to get into this room to stop them. I looked around again but saw no sign of her.

"You're up in half an hour. Make it interesting. This is a huge deal for the boss." The security guard patted me on the shoulder, bringing me back to my purported assignment—the dance. I grabbed a spot in the circular seating area reserved for guests.

"Ladies and gentlemen, please take your seats as we are about to begin the countdown to our launch."

I knew it then—I was out of time to find her.

Feeling slightly defeated but refusing to accept it, I rose while others made their way to nearby chairs. I approached one of the men in uniform seated by the corner, who wasn't far from me. He appeared to be jamming his fingers hard on the keyboard of a desktop computer, stationed in front of him. "Excuse me."

He turned to me with a frown like I was interrupting something important. "Yes?"

I lowered my voice as the lights dimmed and the room quieted down. "There are two of us who are supposed to be...dancers...tonight. But my partner isn't here yet, and you're about to begin so I need to make a call. Do you have a phone I could use?"

A guest sitting close snuffed at me for breaking his concentration. I ignored him, returning my focus to the man in uniform. "Sir, I'm not sure what you're supposed to do here tonight, but phones are not allowed inside here." He made to return to what he was doing, maximizing an open webpage with one click. Insistent on getting the help I wanted, I tapped his arm lightly, and his frown deepened.

But I smiled instead. "Can I use your PC to send an email then? You really don't want the big boss to get half a performance and be angry because you didn't let me contact my partner, do you?" Fear spread across his eyes, and I imagined Pete Zendel must be a real terror around here. Had Red met him yet? I swallowed, not wanting to think how that could go.

He turned back to his computer. And while assuming my desperate effort was in vain, I stepped toward my seat.

"Here, use this computer but send your email quickly because we'll be shutting down in five minutes."

I could hardly believe my ears. I nodded and returned, hoping my face remained expressionless. "I won't take more than a minute." I bent over toward his computer and clicked on the browser, but he was still looking at me. "Do you mind?" I said with a smile.

"Oh." He blushed and stepped behind the computer, giving me much-needed privacy. I typed in my email address quickly, aware that he may not stand aloof for too long.

Subject: SOS

Message: I'm alive. Ruby's innocent, and she's missing. Send backup now. Armed guards are here. Send everyone to Cortexe Corp. HQ now. Det. Mike is critically injured. TNR launch is in a few mins with global implications.

Godspeed.

-Robert Towers.

I addressed it to the captain then hit the Send button. The man glanced up at me, and I smiled. "Almost done, buddy. It's gonna be a big dance tonight." He was about to come around so I used my body to shield the message while it sent. "What a nice cover you've got there." I pointed to the shiny cover on his mouse. Soon the message flashed Sent, and I signed out of my account and then closed the browser while praying someone saw the message in time.

Leaving the desk, I returned to my seat and glanced at the timer. Sixty seconds to launch, the countdown said. I spotted a security guard pointing at me, but I wasn't sure what to do if I was made. I was ready to run, but to where, and without Ruby? Moreover, there was no safe exit that I could see.

"Sir, you're the dancer, right? You're not supposed to be here until after the launch. You have to wait outside," the guard said, urging me to stand.

Whew, for a minute there, I'd thought I was made.

In compliance, I rose, just as a large screen came on. Images of two people standing side by side appeared on the screen. My heart jumped at what I saw. I gasped before I could help myself. The two people who'd appeared were Ruby standing next to a guy who had to be Pete Zendel.

10

BEHOLD, NOW IS THE ACCEPTABLE TIME; BEHOLD NOW IS the day of salvation. -2 Corinthians 6:2

R UBY

The lady guard had been gone for a while when I bent over a bit to look at the edge of the bed. To my dismay, the laser beams at foot level were still on. She'd gone out to try to turn them off, but time was running out fast. Several thoughts ran through my mind, starting with what I should do next. What if she'd gotten caught? What if she couldn't make it back? My stomach tightened at the thought of what could happen to me and to her.

The best I could do now was to sit up and be ready to leave the moment she returned. For the life of me, I couldn't think of her not returning. Or the unimaginable consequences of being stuck here on my own.

I looked toward the window and drew in a calming breath. Nothing but the same bushes was barely visible in the darkness. I laid down, spread my hands over my stomach, and stared at the single light-bulb dangling from the ceiling. The cream-colored ceiling stared back at me, offering me no hope, so I returned to thinking about my options.

If I succeeded in escaping and ran away, how far would my feet carry me before I found help? Or before Cortexe Corp. captured me again?

In the back of the boxlike truck, Robert had said, "Call on the name of Jesus when you reach the end of your ropes," or something like that. I shut my eyes momentarily, contemplating his offer. Then I exhaled deeply, and in my mind, I took a step in that direction. "Jesus..." I said, testing the name on my lips. I figured now was as good a time as any to call on Him.

I had no more room on my ropes right now. First, Robert was gone. And I was stuck here with no way out and no way to stop The New Rulebook. If Pete Zendel's latest threats were true, I also had no future while being under suspicion of murder by the authorities, after being sold lies by Cortexe Corp. There were simply no other options available to me. "Jesus..." I muttered once more and liked the sound of it. After all, saying His name didn't hurt, right? Growing more confident about the efficacy of Jesus' name, I bowed my head slightly and shut my eyes as I'd observed people do in the past.

"Jesus...I call on Your name. Even though I'm not sure You know me, but I'm calling on You anyway. I've done all I can in this situation. Yet I don't see a way out of here or a way out of this. So I need Your help because time is running short. I don't know what fate awaits me out there or in here. Robert is gone...." I choked in a sob.

Then I let go emotionally to Him, with careless abandon. "I've just got...no one else to help me. None to lean on, so I choose to depend on You." I breathed in deeply while feeling as though a ton of bricks had been lifted off me. "Help me out, walk me through into a safe place, Lord Jesus."

A flood of new reality choked my voice further, but I pressed on. "I've never had a family or people to call my own. My only true friend has just died. My other friends have been touch-and-go, go-as-they-come in my life. They move on then cut off, almost like they were never there at all. I'm sometimes scared of what the future holds for me. I'd thought of what life will be like when Robert moves on, marries, and I need to pull away to give them room. Before he died, Robert said he's in love with me. Now, I fear I'm falling in love with the memory of him, the Robert I remember, the one I had with me all this time and didn't know his full worth. He wasn't perfect, but he was good to me. In fact, he was the best I could've asked for. Every smile we shared, even the fights we had, now only drives love for him deeper into my heart.

How can I fall in love with him after he's gone? After he's lost and never to come back. It just feels like a deep hunger that will never find filling."

I wiped away the tears now pouring down my face. It had to be very close to the deadline Pete Zendel had given me, but I didn't care anymore.

"I wish I could get one more chance, if only to tell Robert how much of a blessing he has been to me. How lucky I was to have had him in my life all these years, to have him as my best friend and confidant."

I sighed regretfully, and a frown twisted my face. "I wish I'd understood his conversion to Christianity at the time. At least I should have allowed him to explain what You meant to him instead of shutting him out completely. Please, Lord, I need one more day, just to hear his deep, rich voice and to hear him go high-pitched when he's certain he's annoyed me."

I laughed at the memory with much less angst than I'd felt earlier. Really, it felt so silly now to have been angry at Robert for any reason I could think of. "I want to hear him call me Red one more time." I laughed again, so heartily that I felt like a bird freed from capture, with my wings spread out wide and ready to soar. The joy welling up from inside me had no comparison, and the freedom it ushered me into contrasted with my present circumstances of captivity.

I was shocked, as it felt as though I was talking to Jesus face to face and eye to eye. Like He'd opened up to me as I opened up to Him. Like the more I spilled out the burden inside me, the more of His joy, peace, and freedom I received. Nothing had changed physically, but so much had changed inside me.

Thank you so much, Robert, for giving me Jesus! Suddenly, I grew hungry for more, more of Him, more of this exchange, more of what I'd received. Robert had asked me to call on the name of Jesus. But now, I'd done more than that: I'd thrown myself into Jesus' arms, rolling in His love that couldn't be measured. I felt so loved, so wanted, so appreciated, so treasured that I could hardly put it into words. Something had definitely changed inside me. I might not be able to name it yet, but I loved it, every bit of it. After all, you couldn't name a sweet feeling and you couldn't name a happy experience, you simply lived it. I swung my arms wide, throwing up my feet in the air in ecstatic freedom.

Then voices swelled outside, drawing me back to the present danger I still faced. A creak sounded as the doorknob slowly turned. Bright light from the hallway streamed in like a slice of pie. I was hopeful that it could be the female guard. I figured maybe she made it after all.

I glanced toward the bed's rims to check and saw the laser beams were still on. I was confused, but I assumed she couldn't disable it so she'd returned. My shoulders drooped with disappointment as I'd held high hopes that she would succeed. Nevertheless, I gave her credit for trying, for taking such a huge risk on my behalf. She seemed like a good person inside, despite who she worked for, so I definitely wouldn't forget her help. Then I realized she never even told me her name.

Just then, someone held the door open a little, and I heard some feet shuffling outside while approaching. Then they stopped. Next, a security guard swung the door wide.

I rose to a sitting position, hands looped eagerly, but no longer tense. Whatever news she had, I was ready to take it—good or bad. Another guard stepped into the room, and I was bothered. Then another entered. And yet a third. Why were so many guards returning with her? Did she tell them I was trying to escape? I swallowed, but so much had changed in the past hour, such that I couldn't begin to explain it all if I tried.

Give him the die, I heard somewhere deep inside me.

Was it God speaking to me? That couldn't be. He wouldn't ask me to give up my only leverage. Maybe I was plain out of it right now. I breathed in deeply once more to steady my nerves for whatever was coming. I still hadn't seen her walk through yet, but I could make out the sound of male voices getting closer. Undoubtedly, if she told them I was attempting an escape, Pete Zendel would kill me. Surprisingly, none of that scared me. In fact, I felt so much peace inside me, so much that it was tough for me to understand. With a steeled resolve, I decided that—if it was over for me, if I was going down, then I would go down with God at my side.

The men glanced toward the door then stood at

an attention. Pete Zendel himself made an entrance, his dark glasses impossible to mistake. "Hello, Ruby. The time's up. Let's go."

His men disabled the laser beam with a click, and I stepped one foot tentatively on the floor, then the other. *Give him the die,* I heard again. This time I was certain that it was not coming from my mind.

11

WHEN THE ENEMY SHALL COME IN LIKE A FLOOD, THE Spirit of the Lord shall lift up a standard against him - Isaiah 59:19[NKJV]

As I was led out of the room, I did the one thing that I knew would work when all else failed—I prayed. *Dear Jesus, please take care of me. I commit myself into Your hand.* Prayers seemed to be coming out of me more often and very easily, as though I was having a simple conversation. I didn't care what he did, but I was determined that this monster would definitely not see a sign of weakness from me.

We got on the elevator and rode up to the X floor. Then we walked past the room full of workers in black and white uniform. We entered another elevator, and when it opened, we arrived at Pete Zendel's now-familiar office.

In contrast to the quiet outside, his office buzzed like a worker bee colony. People were running around frantically, clutching papers in their hands, while some were standing next to something in the middle of the room. His office seemed very different from when I'd first stepped in here just hours ago. Huge round bolts held fast a false electronic wall, stuck to the entire left side. Two other sides of the room had been turned into operational electronic stations, with two young men manning each one. Lighting was dim at the corners, though the center of the room was well lit. The desk and chairs I'd seen earlier were gone and had been replaced by a gigantic machine, the size of a refrigerator which was now sitting at the room's center. It was transparent like it was made with glass-ware, though wires of all colors looped across each other, and the wires were visible externally. An empty square hole occupied the middle.

"Get me the cube," Pete Zendel ordered one of his men, who scrambled to do his bidding. He stood by me next to the machine as they turned their attention to a large security monitor mounted high up on the wall. I followed their gaze to the image on the monitor. It was the room I had observed from the COO's office with steel doors, which had a guard stationed in front of it.

Zendel walked over to me, and he stopped, nodding at nothing in particular. "Your new friend, she crossed me by attempting to deactivate the alarms so I made sure it never happens again."

As I realized he was referencing the female guard, I gasped while my hands flew up to my lips in disbelief at what he must have done to her. My heart broke all over again—caused by *this* same man. I observed the mockery dancing in his eyes while hot tears brimmed in mine. He had killed her—and he was gloating about it! How dare he! I remembered my determination not to show weakness to him, so instead of reacting, I straightened to full height. With a finger, I pushed away stray hair from my face and wet my dry lips, but I said nothing.

Getting no reaction from me to his words, he returned his attention to the security monitor. At this point, I could hardly breathe. Furious, I wondered what made him think he could do whatever he wanted with anyone and get away with it? What made him think he could just kill people without consequences?

With The New Rulebook largely operational soon, he'd be unstoppable—possibly untouchable by the law. I could barely imagine his pure reign of brutality! People were asleep in their beds, oblivious that The New Rulebook would forever alter their lives within a few minutes from now.

Why give him the die? I asked God in my heart. *Robert lost his life protecting this die from his hands. It was the last thing he asked me not to yield. Now, I'm just supposed to hand it over to Pete Zendel, without a fight?*

Even while I asked this to God, it felt like the very

hands of God held the reins of my resisting heart, prodding me to release the die. My jaw rose in obstinacy. No. It couldn't be God asking me to do this! Not with everything *I* knew. But, did God know much more than I did? I wasn't ready to consider that option.

The sent guard arrived at the steel doors and briefly discussed with the positioned guard. Then they walked closer to the doors, and one of them keyed in some codes. The huge steel doors parted, and the guard stepped inside, disappearing from screen view.

Moments later, he returned with something cradled in his hand. A square-shaped object sitting inside a casing that seemed to be about the size of the hole in the machine. Some of his men in the room broke into sudden smiles as the positioned guard handed the object to the sent guard—mission accomplished. The positioned guard locked down the steel doors again. Then he moved away but with a more relaxed pose than before. I watched as he paced leisurely until he stopped at the same spot where he'd met up with the sent guard. The sent guard's image slid off the screen's view as he made his return trip.

In readiness for the sent guard's arrival, Pete Zendel walked to a computer screen and began typing something in, pausing every few moments. After a while, the sent guard emerged in person, reentering the room, with their prize in hand, and Zendel waved him over.

He approached, and I saw that the object was

cube-shaped, white in color with five black dots on the one side facing me. It was exactly like the building itself, and just like the cube which was hidden in my earring, except this cube was about twenty times larger than what I had in my possession.

Zendel received it and set it down. He then removed his dark glasses and his voice alteration piece. I saw his eyes for the first time, and it was exactly the same face and brown eyes as Violet—a carbon copy—as the lady guard had said. The only difference was that his eyes were chilly as ice.

I couldn't help the thought that truly, the monster was shedding his mask and showing his true color. He glanced at me briefly then focused his attention again on the cube. He lifted it, inspecting it with much glee. Then he turned around, eyes locked on me where I stood. I didn't panic at all. Instead, I prayed silently in my heart.

God, I now choose to obey You even though I don't understand. You know my loss, my sacrifice, and my pain. I want to stop Pete Zendel, for Robert's sake, so his death is not in vain, but You know best. Please stop this evil man somehow in Jesus' name, amen.

With this heartfelt prayer, I immediately felt the responsibility for stopping Pete Zendel shift from my shoulders to the only One who could actually do it best. Relieved, I stepped back even as the frenzy around me increased.

Zendel observed his men around the room, then the cube, and then he smacked his lips delightfully like he was about to consume a delicious meal. He laughed, and it sounded to me like a broken piece of guitar with every quack he cracked. Then his focus shifted to me, and his laughter dried up as hatred filled his cold eyes. He set the cube down gently. I figured that it was either he hated me, my calm posture, or both.

As though reading my thoughts, he strode over to me, his gaze holding mine. "You have something that belongs to me, and I want it back—now."

I shrugged, but my eyes stayed focused. "You know what, Pete? To me, it feels strange how I can stare into the same kind of eyes in two days and experience them very differently. You may look like Violet, but your resemblance is purely physical, as I can see no commonality between who you two really are."

The apparent threat in his eyes was unquestionable. He wouldn't ask me twice. So, in obedience to God, I unhooked my right earring, then broke off the golden die I'd glued to it to keep it safe with me at all times. Then I handed it over to him, losing my last shred of a bargaining chip. My heart quaked, and it felt like I'd just betrayed Robert, and even as though I'd betrayed the world too.

"Good." He reached out and accepted the small die and handed it to the closest guard. "Fill it in."

The guard crossed over to the large cube, hefting it slightly. Lights clicked on as soon as he inserted the golden die into a tiny hole at the base. They blinked rapidly as he lifted the entire composition, carrying it toward the machine.

The guard stopped in front of the machine and looked at Pete Zendel, awaiting fresh commands.

"Place it in. I need this to launch now."

The guard pushed the cube into the square hole within the machine's core. Seconds passed. Then a light blinked. And then another and another. Within moments, the machine started humming, and blue lights turned on piece by piece until it cast a hue over the entire room. Why did everything they touched here blink when they weren't traffic wardens?

Zendel strode toward a small desk, his men at attention as he approached, forcefully prodding me along beside him. He pointed forward. "Turn on the camera. It's time to bring our guests on."

Two of his men hurried to a tripod stand, with a camera sitting atop it, rotating. They pulled a remote from its base, then pushed a white bar on it. The camera focused, with our faces reflecting on it.

He glanced at me, beckoning one of his guards closer. "Bring her here."

Two muscular men approached, taking me by the arm and standing me right next to Zendel, with only inches apart. I didn't know why, but maybe it was to keep a close eye on me. Regardless, I remained calm, but I felt thirsty all of a sudden. My eyelids drooped heavy like I hadn't slept in ages. I took a deep breath, struggling to retain my focus.

To the left side of the wall, a wide screen came on.

"Welcome and thanks for joining us for this momentous occasion. As you know, we have been working hard on this project for a long time. We had some...technical issues in the past, which I'm happy to announce to you, that we've now sorted out. Tonight, in fact right now, The New Rulebook is being activated." He pressed a button on the machine, speaking into it, and then scanning his eyes.

"Welcome to The New Rulebook," a pleasant feminine voice announced, and it printed those words over the large display screen. That welcome was followed by images of what could probably be hundreds of surveillance cameras in small square images, dotting the screen. An analysis section, like a ribbon at the edge of the screen, began scrolling out individual and company names, then governments and their national symbols, indicating their probability percentage of deviation.

I couldn't believe my eyes. I watched in shock as it was actively searching databases, looking up people and providing their exact location. It was even using voice scans, and it found people *anywhere* in the world. Violet was right. There was no hiding from it. Proposed actions against each entity corresponded alongside each name.

Applause rang out across the room.

"Ladies and gentlemen, as you can see, our launch of The New Rulebook is successful," Zendel announced to my dismay.

More cheers followed, including some shouting from his guards. A wide grin spread out across his face, and his eyes gleefully swept through the audience with pride. In contrast, my heart threatened to explode out of my chest as I helplessly watched. *Oh no! This can't possibly be happening!* Nothing compared to my despair right now. I choked, and it was like a movie was playing on rewind, as my mind browsed the events leading up to this moment. It started with the routine delivery turned not so routine, followed by Violet's death. Then me dragging Robert into this situation and getting him killed, then Ms. Bryant, and running away from my own home, and then lastly, this lady guard whom Pete Zendel had killed for attempting to help me. I'd lost everything. All for *this*. All for The New Rulebook!

I turned my eyes away to lessen the hurt, as a dull aching pain twirled deep within me, sapping my worn strength even further.

Then for no apparent reason, the room went silent. All the humming ceased, leaving only human voices.

"What just happened?" Pete Zendel belted out, so I flipped around to see what was going on.

Before my eyes, an "error" message flashed repeatedly on the large screen. The print was bold and unmistakable. Then another message appeared soon after saying, "shutting down software."

I blinked twice to be sure. Yes, I was seeing correctly. There it was, really shutting down. I could hardly believe it!

Eyes wide, I chuckled in victory. Then I smiled broadly. God did it—like I'd prayed He would—but in

His own way. Now I knew. The golden die was not designed to complete The New Rulebook; it was made to destroy it. Pete Zendel got the ten percent he asked for!

He turned to me, glaring with unbridled fury.

"What did you do?!" He rushed at me, his arms extended. When I dodged and stepped sideways, he regained his balance and came at me again. "Arrhhh!" His arms were aiming for my neck in a viselike manner.

Suddenly, the room exploded with light. Zendel got knocked off his feet just as white smoke billowed in from the door. Force from the explosion threw me hard against the wall, then smoke filled my lungs. I sucked in air, gasping for oxygen.

"Pete Zendel, freeze! MPD!" They rushed at him with him still lying on the ground. They were all wearing gas and facemasks as bright lights from their headgear pinned onto our faces. Zendel turned away, covering his face with his hands. He tried to rise, but they forced him to remain where he was. "Stay down, or we'll use force, Zendel!" They held him down to the ground.

My eyes crossed to the error message, which was still flashing on the screen. I was speechless. I was rooted to the spot as officers cuffed Zendel's hands behind his back.

"Pete Zendel, you are under arrest. You'll be going away for a very long time." Another officer read him his rights, though I doubted he deserved any.

Contented, I raised myself off the floor, pushing up with my elbow. My eyes stung with the white tear gas, and the strong odor of smoke choked me, so I coughed repeatedly. My poor attempt to stave off the smoke burning through my lungs, using my hands, had been a waste as I still gasped for air, but I'd remained to see Pete Zendel arrested and cuffed.

Officers now flooded the room we were in, apprehending the armed guards next. Their attention turned to the large machine, which, thankfully, was still as dead as when it went down minutes ago.

"Thank you, dear Jesus," I muttered.

I rose to my feet and stumbled out of the room. Most officers ignored me, probably because I was unarmed. Some officers walked Pete Zendel, in handcuffs, past me, and he met my gaze and smiled coldly.

"Keep moving, mister," the officer holding him ordered, forcing him to move past me. I was about to exit when an officer accosted me, staring a little too closely at me and invading my space.

"Excuse me, ma'am?" he said when he was close enough.

I frowned, but I stopped. "Yes, officer, can I help you?" I was still wiping the tears that were streaming down my cheeks due to the smoke's sting, so it wasn't really a convenient time to be having a conversation.

"Are you Ruby Masters?" he asked.

I gaped. *How on earth did he know...?* I nodded, but I didn't say a word.

"Do you know Robert Towers?" he asked, this time, more slowly.

I hesitated. "Yes, I...I knew him."

My heart missed a beat. *What was this about?*

"What name does he alone call you?" he pressed further, unperturbed by my lack of interest.

I exhaled exaggeratedly since, now, he had really gone too far. There were things that stayed between Robert and me, and what he used to call me when he was alive would now be one of them. Moreover, all these questions and talk of Robert was bringing back painful memories.

The officer glanced in the direction he'd just come from then back at me. "I don't have much time, but I need to verify who you are, please." He checked his watch impatiently. "I've got ten seconds to get an answer."

I gave him a measured look then and wondered what the risk of telling him could be. Since Robert was dead, it didn't matter to anyone else but me anymore. Who cared what he called me? So, I sighed and answered him. "Red. He called me Red."

Then he pulled out a radio and spoke into it. "The package is secured alive. I repeat: the package is secured alive."

I jolted. "Wait, who sent you?"

He extended me a hand, inviting me to go with him. "Sergeant Towers."

Sergeant Towers...? I swallowed and stopped frozen in my tracks. I suddenly felt faint, and dizziness set in. I held a hand to my stomach to stabilize myself. "Robert's dead. I saw him die." It had to be the smoke messing with my head. I must be hearing things now.

If this was a dream, I needed to wake up—and fast too.

The officer took me by the hand and guided me toward the elevator. "No, ma'am. Sergeant Robert Towers is alive, and he's waiting for you outside the main gate."

12

FOR I KNOW THE PLANS THAT I HAVE FOR YOU, DECLARES the Lord, plans ... to give you a future and a hope. -Jeremiah 29:11

The last few days had taught me one thing— that the creases of life are what make us human. Rough turns and twists and disappointments carve our core values. As I followed the officer out of the large Cortexe Corp. main building, anticipation of a reunion mounted within me. Absentmindedly, I tapped an impatient hand repeatedly on my thigh as a longing for quicker reunion welled up deeply, tough to put into words. A cautious chuckle escaped my lips as I realized that so much had happened since Robert and I parted hours ago. Much had changed, but yet some other things remained the same.

"The chopper's ready to medevac. Hurry it up," someone came through on the radio.

"Copy that. We're almost with you."

Medevac who? Robert? My heart skipped another beat as I stepped forward faster to ask the officer what condition Robert was in, but then on second thought, I drew back. I would rather see him for myself.

My heart fluttered, but I stilled the panic rising inside me, shutting down the voice in my head saying that it was worse to reunite with Robert only to watch him die.

The officer and I burst out through the outer doors, walking against the officers streaming in. Scores of flashing police headlights greeted us at the outer compound.

We strode toward the main gate. Outside the partly-opened gates, the tail of a waiting helicopter stuck out. I wanted to run to it, but I restrained myself. *One step at a time, Ruby.* But at least my pace increased along with the officer's upon nearing the main gate. If Robert needed medical evacuation, I'd run to save time. But, I wondered, how did he survive the explosion I had seen with my own very eyes? How did he get the police here just in time, if that was his doing? I couldn't figure that out, so instead, I breathed slowly to calm my nerves. I had so much to tell Robert, and a lot of ground to cover in catching up. But I was grateful. I had asked God for one more chance with him, and if this was it, then I would show my gratitude by not complaining about his health condition, whatever it was.

Soon, we exited the Cortexe Corp. main entry gate, and by then, I was trembling from head to toe, helpless to stop it. I wrapped my arms around myself for stability, but my mind wouldn't keep itself from wondering about the possibilities that waited. What if Robert's injuries were so bad that he couldn't even hear, speak, or comprehend? What if he was—*Stop it, Ruby. Seriously.*

I refused to think any further about worse conditions he could be in. Instead, I involuntarily gripped the hem of my shirt as I broke into a frenzied half run. I was still imagining possible scenarios when we closed in on the chopper. My hair thrashed carelessly around my shoulders, flipping onto my face with each step. My breath came in gasps the closer we got. My left hand wound tightly with a forceful grip on the side zipper of my shirt as my desperation rose to fever pitch. "God, please, I don't want to see him die. Please save Robert's life, I beg You. Please, Jesus." My heart was wringing with both anticipation and dread as I tried to hold my peace outwardly. We reached the chopper, and I placed a hand over my heart with my breath heaving uncontrollably.

Someone tapped on my shoulder from behind. "Thank God you're okay, Ruby."

I froze in my steps, gasping aloud as the rich, deep voice of Robert Towers soared into my ears.

I flipped around. Then I stepped back, eyes popping out of their sockets, with my mouth agape. True to my ears, I gazed into the emerald-green eyes I now loved.

"Robert?" I whispered through a choked voice while my feet were still rooted in shock. "What? How did you survive? I mean—" I was pretty sure I wasn't making much sense. Tears broke through the corners of my eyes, dropping gladly down my cheeks. I made no attempt whatsoever to wipe them. Instead, I let out a held breath as relief poured through me.

"Ruby—" he said breathlessly.

"Red," I cut in with a hoarse laugh. "Call me Red, Robert," I repeated, ensuring he heard me right.

But even saying that felt like a chore. There was one thing we both wanted—and needed—to do right now. I saw it clearly in his eyes as tears rolled down his cheeks too. For someone who didn't cry, I knew that was a pretty big deal. We rammed straight into each other's arms, gripping each other like a key to a lock, and sobbing.

The medic blanket draped over his shoulder cascaded to the ground, but we held onto each other still. We turned on the waterworks as our sobs mingled into unintelligible sounds. I felt every wave of emotion in these tears. Pain, regret, relief, joy, love, and finally, peace as our sobs quieted moments later and we parted.

"I thought you were dead. Then they told me you were alive, and then something about being mede-vacked. So I thought the worst." I sensed some distance from him even though he held onto my hands. I said nothing, as I was just glad to have him be alive.

"It's not me. It's a detective who was killed with me

—well, sort of. He is badly injured, but I did the best I could to keep him conscious long enough before help arrived." He looked me over.

"We need to go right away." I tapped his arm lightly. "We stopped The New Rulebook."

He smiled then nodded. "I know. The way I heard it, *you* stopped The New Rulebook. Good work."

I hesitated, not sure this was the right time, but I was determined not to accept credit for what I didn't do, especially what I fought not to do. "Actually, God stopped The New Rulebook, Robert. I just happened to be in the room."

He tucked stray hair off my face, to behind my ears. "You were very brave standing in the same room with a monster, Red. That makes you a hero in my book."

I swallowed as I saw that he was still not getting the point. Plus, I wasn't sure how to break it to him or even how to start. I simply settled for the easiest point. "I have a lot to tell you, Robert."

His face straightened, and then he exhaled. "Me too, Red. Me too."

I wrapped my arms around myself as cool wind sent shivers over my body.

Robert picked up a black bag I hadn't seen him drop. Then he guided me toward the chopper with a hand gently placed on my back. Military medics were attempting to lift someone onto the chopper with a stretcher, all seemingly talking at the same time. It had to be Robert's friend.

"Is he okay?"

Robert seemed worried, but he sounded cheerful. "He's a strong guy. He'll pull through. C'mon, let's get in." Police officers in the chopper barely paid attention as Robert helped me up inside. Another helicopter landed, this time within the Cortexe Corp. compound, bringing in more cops. I held onto a hand support belt as I was seated opposite Robert. The cramped space bothered me only a little since the only thing I wanted was to leave this place.

"Your eyes, you need some sleep, Red." When I looked up at Robert, he signaled a laid-down position with his hands clapped together and planted sideways against his cheek, assuming that I hadn't heard him, since the helicopter's blades were whirring louder to increased speed.

I gave him a thumbs-up. It was now impossible for him to hear me above the noise. The stretcher with his friend on it was secured to large floor rings next to me. The injured detective looked peacefully asleep to all the buzz around him, completely cut off from this world. I swallowed and wondered. *It could have been Robert.* Gratitude overwhelmed me afresh. Across from me, Robert's strong oval face, though tired, assured me he was really here—and he was fine. I exhaled in pure relief as the pilot began his ascension and Cortexe Corp. permanently fell to a blur behind us.

∽

We arrived at the Mercy Memorial Hospital decking to emergency lights shining around a wide circle, identifying our place to set the chopper down. Medical personnel clad in white coats, overalls, and plain blue scrubs surrounded the landing pad like ants, each standing on their toes, waiting to meet us as soon as we touched the ground. Medics on the chopper unlatched the hooks from the floor ring boards, lifting the stretcher with the detective on it. We alighted next from the chopper and stood close to the stretcher while a chopper medic, who appeared to be the lead, approached the hospital team.

"We've got a patient with severe trauma to his neck and arms, plus burn injuries. BP is one ninety-six over one thirty, and he's in critical condition...." An oxygen hand mask was placed over his nose and mouth by hospital medics on the ground, manually pressing the bag attached to it at regular intervals to help his breathing. A fresh blanket was also placed over him.

Robert took the previous one, handing it to the chopper medics.

A nurse, who looked as flustered as a newbie, was scrawling the furious tumble of information being spat out by the chopper medics onto a writing pad. Her chest rose and fell in quick breaths accelerating faster than the chopper's blades. Strong altitude winds flipping her pages weren't helping either.

"Commence CPR!" a medic in a white coat

shouted, so I presumed he must be the doctor in charge.

Another rushed forward and began stumping on the detective's chest with both of his palms linked together in counted spurts, while others lifted the detective simultaneously onto a Gurney from the stretcher, wheeling him speedily toward the hospital mains.

Strong wind pushed our clothing and forced them to stick tighter to our bodies, while I used a hand to shield my eyes. My hair whipped carelessly into empty space, but I noticed that Robert stuck close to me as though I'd disappear if he blinked. I smiled because I worried about him the same way now.

We barely spoke during the twenty-minute flight, but reassuring glances between us confirming that we were both alive and well was enough. There would be plenty of time for us to talk later.

"Are you okay?" he asked as we approached the main hospital facility on foot, heading toward the elevators. Worry lines crinkled his forehead.

I nodded. "Yes, I'm fine. I'm just a little tired, that's all."

He still kept his gaze on me, scanning my face. "Did they do...anything...to you?"

It took a moment for it to register in my mind what he was really asking, and very politely so.

I shook my head. "No. Nothing happened. I mean, between him and me, and I'm grateful for that." His shoulders relaxed. "What about you? Are you hurt? Do you need medical attention?"

He shrugged. "Now that I've seen you're all right, nothing hurts anymore. I just need a good shower and some sleep."

I punched his arm playfully. "Oh, that didn't hurt?"

He laughed, grabbing the tail of my shirt, and pulling me back as I attempted to flee. "Why don't we see whether it did?" He swung me around, and I faced his bare, well-toned chest, muscles rippling with every move. Like a magnet, the sudden strong desire to touch them enveloped me out of nowhere. I quickly looked away and took a step back, biting my lower lip. Oh, I was in real trouble. I was not just in love with the memory of Robert Towers anymore; I was currently, presently in love with *him*.

～

We sat outside the waiting area of the hospital while the detective underwent surgery. Several burns he'd sustained were already treated en route to the hospital. I looked at the clock on the wall and saw that we'd been here for about two hours, and other officers were now gone, leaving Robert and me.

I walk past the pharmacy prescription pickup area, a yawn escaping my lips while I struggled to keep my eyes open and alert. Two teenagers—male and female—one wearing a tee shirt and baggy pants, the other a midriff top and yellow skin-tight leggings, played music from a mobile device, louder than their earbuds required. What was really loud as speakers were their voices arguing over who owned an item they apparently just won over the air. I wondered why they were here. Nevertheless, I strode past them.

I approached the nursing station and saw a nurse giving instructions while standing behind three other nurses. Her hair was dyed bright blue, and loop earrings on both her ears dangled all the way down her neck, touching her shoulders. Her overdone red lipstick appeared too much for a hospital environment. But she didn't seem to care what anyone thought—and she looked like she was in charge. The other nurses, whose faces were somber, scurried to carry out her instructions. Plastic transparent boxes— all labeled and stacked one on top of the other and containing diverse medications—sat on a higher table behind her.

"Excuse me," I said as I approached.

Her earrings jingled as she spun toward me, placing some prescription sheets onto a tray and handing it to one of the nurses without a glance. She offered me a studied smile, long lashes batting, but she said nothing.

"Can I please have a shirt for my friend? He was in an accident earlier today and doesn't have any clothes."

She considered me with a measured look, scanning me from head to toe. She narrowly glanced at some place behind her and then settled her gaze again on me once more. "Sure. We can definitely find something." She rose and walked over to a door marked Staff Closet then returned with a blue outfit in hand. "We don't have regular clothes on hand, but he can manage the top of scrubs if you'd like." She handed the scrub to me; her long nails painted purple, each with white-dotted tips, met mine.

I looked the top over, spreading it out wide, and checking its size. "Yes, that will do." I smiled at her. "Thank you very much."

She folded the bottom piece, placing it on her desk. "You're welcome. I hope your friend feels better."

Hmmm...she's much nicer than I'd assumed from a distance. I nodded. Then I walked back to Robert, and as I approached, I saw his head was bent forward. He didn't even seem to notice my approach. "Robert?"

When he looked up, his face wore a tired grin. His eyes were puffy around the edges, and he was looking worn out. He rubbed a lazy hand over his face.

"Here." I offered him the top scrub.

He accepted it, turning the right side out. "Oh, thanks a lot." He smiled, sighing gratefully, then slipped it on in a singular motion.

Robert had been thanking me and apologizing for every little thing since we arrived at the hospital, in fact since we reunited. But if he knew my real intentions for giving him this shirt was more than simply to cover his bare chest, he might not be so thankful. I cringed and tried to focus on a point past his head. Still, I felt his eyes set on me.

"You look tense. Are you sure you don't want me to rub your shoulders? It might help you relax."

Heat rose to my cheeks, and thankfully, I was still on my feet. "No thanks. I think I'm going to go grab a cup of coffee at the cafeteria. I'll be back." I took a couple of steps toward the elevator, but he inched forward in his seat.

"I'll come with you."

I waved him back. How did I make him know I was actually trying to get away from *him*? I stopped, then massaged my neck in thought. *Wow, he was right. I am tense!* But I had to keep him from following me. "Robert, I'm not going to disappear, I promise. I'll be right back." I could've added that I had issues, feelings to be exact, to sort out, but instead I cited that inwardly.

I was relieved when he sat back down, yawning, while with one hand he rubbed the stub of his new beard. For someone who was usually clean-shaven, he didn't look bad at all.

Shaking my head, I resumed my trip to the cafeteria. But something about his pose, a certain vulnerability he rarely showed, stopped me in my tracks. So I took a couple of steps back to him. This time, his face was cupped in both of his hands, while he leaned out of his chair a little.

"Robert?"

He turned to me. Then a smile lit his face.

"It's going to be okay. We're going to be fine." I offered a tentative smile in return, gently rubbing his arm. Color spread across his cheeks as he blushed up to his ears. I withdrew my hands and looked away too, so as not to embarrass him.

But he reached for my hand, squeezing it gently. "It's all right, Red. You don't have to look away. I'm sorry. It's involuntary, but don't worry about it. They are my feelings, and so they're my problem."

My heart wrenched—but was it from guilt or from confusion? I wasn't sure, so I took my hands back. "I'm going to get some coffee," I managed to say before half walking, half running and hightailing it out of there.

I sat in the hospital cafeteria, cupping the freshly brewed cup of coffee in my hand. Standing to my left, a mother and her daughter murmured about the condition of their father who was in the ER. The daughter looked distraught, but her mother looked like she had completely lost hope. Concerned, I wanted to reach over and encourage her, but that would mean revealing that I'd been eavesdropping. The mother finally managed a thin smile. Then she took her daughter's hand and squeezed it.

The precious sight tugged at my heart, so I looked away and shifted the Styrofoam cup to my other hand rather than setting it down on the Formica table.

Patrons formed a beeline around the register, all waiting patiently, though fraught with long faces, and their thoughts dwelt miles away.

An elderly couple walked over and sat next to me so I scooted over to allow them more room. The man opened an envelope, and the woman's shoulders were visibly tense as she looked at him seeming expectant but also hesitant.

He read the letter. Then he turned to her. "They said it's heartburn, not a heart attack. His EKG came out okay. Grandpa's going to be fine."

She hugged him and then let out a sob, with a hand over her mouth. She turned to me. "He's my dad."

I nodded to them. Then I smiled, hoping it communicated my concern for them well enough.

Soon, they both rose and walked over to the buffet area for some food.

I leaned my head against the headrest and closed my eyes. Clanging dishware rang into my ears, announcing the workers and chefs behind short ceramic boulders were creating dishes that made my mouth water. But I had a problem bigger than hunger, a more personal matter going on inside.

I hadn't prayed since we arrived at the hospital, though I longed to. This new faith was so good, but I felt I needed full focus when I found the time to pray. Having Robert here had been a joy but also distracting, to say the least. Knowing he was alive was definitely a relief. But everything had changed, and I couldn't ignore that. When I thought he was dead, all I had to figure out was dealing with the loss and the developing feelings I had for him, which were never there before. Although I was happy that he was alive and that he was here—but he still had feelings for me, and that tied me in a bind.

It's funny to think that, with the distance I had

sensed from him when we first reunited, I actually thought those feelings he had for me must've died in the explosion at Cortexe Corp. Now that I knew they were still alive and kicking, where could I begin unraveling this? How did I know *other* things hadn't changed on his end—feelings aside? I couldn't figure this out alone, and this was definitely something I needed to talk to Jesus about. I opened my eyes, straightening for another sip. But the warmth was gone, and the drink tasted lukewarm and even bland too. I set the cup on the table, now finished with its contents.

They are my feelings, so they're my problem, Robert had just said upstairs. What did that mean for us? Were we staying in the friend's zone? What did I do about the feelings *I* was now having? I sighed and noted that I had all these questions and no answers— yet. As though in response, a sudden ache developed along my jawline so I rubbed it absentmindedly.

"Hey. I thought I'd find you here. Sorry, I got worried when you didn't come back for half an hour."

His familiar deep voice sounded behind me, sending butterflies down my stomach. I'd never reacted to his voice this way—ever. What was going on with me? *Get a grip, Ruby.*

"It's pretty nice down here. Now I see why you stayed back. All these pretty flowers and enticing food aroma could capture one's senses...."

I whisked around as though I'd been caught with a hand in the forbidden cookie jar. I tried to smile, but it came out crooked. "I was just catching a breather."

He grabbed a spot next to me and sat down.

I gasped at the bruises on his neck and on the back of his head. "Robert, you're injured! You need a doctor," I shouted, even before I realized it.

He rubbed his neck lightly. Then he shrugged. "Ah, it's not a big deal. It will go away on its own."

But I wasn't accepting that excuse. I rose snappily, refusing to let him dissuade me, and his eyebrows arched. "No, Robert. I didn't get you back only to lose you again. We're going to see a doctor. As in, now."

He winced playfully but didn't get up.

But I wasn't fooled. "I'm not taking no for an answer, Emerald Eyes."

He looked up sharply, a pleasant surprise written on his face. "You have no idea how much I've missed hearing that." Those dazzling green eyes grew misty. "I'm so glad you're here and so glad you're okay." He looked away, then rose to his feet. "All right, you got it. Let's go see your doctor friends, so I can get back here for my cup of tea." He pointed at me, jokingly. "Now, let's be honest, if you were the one, you'd *never* accept to see a nurse's assistant, let alone a doctor, Red. You know I'm right."

Of course, he was right, but his protest fell on deaf ears. I just knew that I was not risking losing him again. Not when there was ready help.

We took the stairs to the waiting area instead, since the wait for the elevator was taking longer than usual. I was relieved that the issue of our feelings was relegated to the back burner—for now.

◦∼◦

"What's going on, sergeant? The newspapers this morning said you're dead. Are you dead or not? I don't need confusion here," the captain barked playfully. It was nice to see a laidback side to Robert's boss who was always formal in his conversations.

Laughter filtered through the speakerphone, and Robert and I smiled. "Thanks for the promotion, boss. The death news about me is from Cortexe Corp. before we took them down. But I'm very much alive, and I've got Ruby here with me. You should know she was key to the successful takedown."

Static crackled through.

"So, you're both okay? By the way, Ruby, your name has been cleared in the Violet Zendel case, but we'll need your statement on record."

I nodded, and then remembered he was on the phone. "Sure. Thank you, sir, for clearing me. Yes, I'm ready to provide my testimony of what I saw and experienced."

My name had been cleared? Oh, thank You, Jesus!

"Towers, if you're still at the hospital, check on Detective Mike Argan before you leave. I want to know his status. He's a good man."

Robert nodded, just like I'd done before he then spoke. "Yes, sir. I'll do so."

"From the look of things out here, you two are now celebrities of a sort. They've got a lot of media folks lurking at the hospital entrance, just waiting to get a glimpse of the two people who took down a behemoth of a company."

What? Media was here? How did they know about us and Cortexe Corp. when it had barely been a couple of hours? News sure traveled quickly.

"Sir, in that case, we'll need a ride home," Robert inserted.

"No, actually, we booked two hotel rooms for you both at the Highland Residence Hotel downtown because you can't go back home yet. Moreover, the media has camped outside your places, and we're still combing through both apartments searching for explosives and any possible surveillance materials. That's going to take a couple of days and maybe even weeks, estimating by my experience."

Robert and I exchanged glances at the update. "Yes, sir," we responded simultaneously.

"I'll send you out a ride when you're ready," the captain said.

Other voices muffled faintly through the line as if he was distracted. "Thank you, sir. We'll go and let you get back to more important things."

Just then, he came back on the line. "By the way, great work on bringing down The New Rulebook. Your insistence was key to a successful mission. Another promotion may be in order if it is approved by the State office." Robert shook my hand excitedly then let go while grinning ear to ear.

He held the phone up higher so I sensed that the call was wrapping up. "Thank you, sir. This was a team effort. Thank you for your leadership."

The line clicked off and the call ended, so Robert handed the phone back to the nurse who'd lent it to us.

I tapped him on the shoulder. "We've got to get new phones, Robert. We can't keep borrowing from strangers."

He nodded, and then turned with his forehead creasing. "Are you sure you can handle the new model phones? For me, I'll stick with the old-school drag-alongs. Nobody monitors you on that."

I guessed that The New Rulebook experience now made Robert wary of technology.

I laughed heartily. "Please get a phone from this century, so I don't feel like I'm talking to an old you coming up in about forty years. The crankiness won't be fun now."

He shrugged and eyed me. "Maybe we should just go back to the letter-writing era. You know, using hard A-five paper, blue-ink pen, dropping a letter in the mailbox, and waiting days for it to arrive at its destination...." Robert's still expression made it hard for me to tell if he was serious about it or not.

I chuckled. Then I patted his arm playfully. "Oh, don't you mean letters to your future self not sending it to someone else in this age and time."

He was silent for some moments. Then he pointed at me. "Oh, you got me nailed." We both laughed heartily. Then we quieted down. "I got a promotion." He looked at me, waving a hand.

I nodded, feeling the same excitement. "My name is cleared. What could be better for us now?"

We took each other's hand. My throat clogged with emotion, and I realized I couldn't keep it in any longer. I peered up at him, gently pulling my hand away. "Robert, something important happened to me while I was held at Cortexe Corp." I waited for his response to know whether to continue the revelation.

His jaw firmed, and he cast me a serious glance. "You've got my attention."

13

WHEN THE LORD BROUGHT BACK THE CAPTIVE ONES OF Zion, we were like those who dream...Psalm 126:1

"So what did they say?" Robert put his scrubs shirt back on, pulling it over his head, and I helped him. "That I'm good to go?" He jumped to his feet, eagerly, from the hospital bed.

"Not so fast, sergeant," I teased. A nurse had kept him on it when I went down to collect his preliminary lab results. She seemed to have an interested eye for him though, but I didn't worry at all. As things were, I was still fighting my own internal war of feelings. I tried to step out of the room, but he insisted I stayed with him, prolonging my emotional torture.

The nurse received the sheet containing his results from me and read it out aloud. "They gave you a clean bill of health. Although your cholesterol is a bit high, so you'll need to watch those numbers." She tapped on the sheet. "They said you should rest for a week or so, and then you're free to get back to work."

I expected to hear an excited response from Robert, but he was silent. When I twisted toward him, I found him staring at me, and my eyes rounded in curiosity.

"Thank you, nurse. Red, please I've got to ask you something."

"You're welcome." The nurse handed back the sheet and stepped out to give us privacy.

When she left, I nodded to him. "Sure. Ask away."

He perched on the edge of the hospital bed with coolness surrounding his frame. But my heart beat wildly, and my fingers were nervously latched together as I was unsure what he was about to ask. Earlier, I'd narrated my conversion to Christ, before the doctor arrived to see him. Tears had streamed down Robert's face as he hugged me, telling me he'd seen the new light in my face from the moment we met near the chopper but that he hadn't known the source. He said he was so happy for me, and that now we could grow in our faith together since his salvation experience was pretty recent too. We agreed to look for more resources on the internet to help us grow, and to find a good fellowship to attend.

The doctor walked into that scene, so he paused and asked us, "I can excuse you two if you need a moment." We both laughed, saying no. But I could see my news had positively impacted him. He was happy, chipper, and moved like he'd been reinvigorated.

My eyes rose to meet his, and that left me wondering if he'd finally seen the *other* news—the news I hadn't told him yet. The courage to share it had eluded me when I had the chance. Moreover, I knew that now being a Christian, I needed to talk to Jesus before talking with Robert, and I hadn't been able to do so yet.

"Yeah, I remember you said you wanted to ask me something?" I rewound our conversation.

"Yes, I did. And please know I'm not asking for any special treatment here. But considering everything that happened, I've missed you so much, and I'd like to spend time with you, if you don't mind. When I thought I lost you out there..." He wiped a nervous hand across his lips. Then his eyes looked at me pleadingly. "Please, Red. Spend one week with me, every day. Then you can go off to Bora Bora if you want. I promise, we'll have fun, go to nice places, and talk. Just you and me for seven days and nothing more."

Okay, our...issues were up from the back burner. My gaze remained glued to the Sweet Cheese Bakery sticker stuck to the side of the nursing tray left on the bedside, and I thought about his offer and how it might change things for us relationship-wise. Was I ready and could I handle it if during that time together, he found out how I now felt about him? But another thought chided me. *You know better than to say no to your best friend who just survived an explosion.* Inside me was turmoil, so I smiled helplessly to ease the silence. "Sure, Emerald Eyes. No problem. Just pick me up at seven in the morning then drop me off at five in the evening, and we should be good."

His eyes rounded as he jumped to his feet and hugged me, but my hands hung limp at my side. "Thank you so much, Red! That sounds perfect. Thank you."

The only thing I kept saying to myself, over and over again was, "Help me, Jesus! *Seven* days alone with him will be hard... even just a couple of hours at this hospital has been a struggle so far. Help me, Jesus."

A nurse entered and flipped a chart. "Sergeant Towers?"

Robert swung around and nodded. "Yes?"

She smiled to us and pointed toward the door. "Your vehicle is here. They asked me to give you both these as well." She handed us hats and sunglasses wide enough to cover our faces to our ears. "Because of the media."

We accepted the items.

"Thank you." Robert shook her hand on our behalf.

But as I looked at it, I shuddered at the dark glasses. They eerily reminded me of Pete Zendel, so I handed mine back to her. "I think the hat will do." When she didn't seem offended, relief washed over me.

As we left the room, we proceeded to the elevators, heading to the hospital's upper level. Detective Mike was out of surgery and now in intensive care so we went up one floor then turned toward the ICU to see him. When we approached a nurse stationed at the service desk, she looked up at us and smiled. "We're here to see Detective Mike, please," Robert said, offering her a smile as well.

She glanced at her screen briefly then picked up a roster, thumbed down a list until her finger stopped near the end. "Yes, he's here, but I'm sorry to inform you that he's currently not receiving visitors due to mild sedation by the doctors."

A worried frown lined Robert's forehead. "Is he all right? I mean, the last we heard—"

The nurse raised a hand, cutting him off. "There are no new issues, sir, but his sedation was only a precaution post-procedure."

Robert and I exchanged glances before I drew closer. "So you're saying he's still going to be all right, right?"

She nodded in affirmation. "Yes, ma'am. That's exactly what his stats show. All things being equal, he's going to be okay. In fact, he should wake up in a few hours. Then we'll continue his treatment and recovery."

Robert exhaled, and his shoulders visibly relaxed. "That sounds good. We'll be back to check on him again tomorrow when he's awake then."

She nodded and settled the roster again on her desk.

"Thank you, ma'am." I smiled, and then we made our way to the hospital exit, hats ready on our heads.

∼

The shopping mall was full of shoppers and wares. But the fresh and frozen strawberries at one stand caught my eye, and I chuckled as I drew closer and inhaled their fragrant aroma. Fresh ones smelled like it and tasted like it. But for me those frozen ones in the freezer section had only the taste. I grabbed one pack of the fresh ones, and my mind shifted to Robert and me. Just like these strawberries, Robert and I had known each other for a long time. But the next seven days, starting today, gave us both aroma and taste—the aroma of fresh opportunities for a new start, and the taste of experiencing and exploring our new faith together.

Luscious fruits jostled for space in my shopping basket, and Robert trailed close behind me.

"What about these apples? Do you think he'll like them?" Robert shrugged, holding out a small pack of three yellowish-green Gala apples.

I smiled and examined them. "Well, he's sick and stuck on a hospital bed so I'm pretty sure he'll love *any* apples we can bring to him."

Robert dropped two more apples into our basket for him and me. "Here. Let me help you with this." He carried the basket from me, lightening up my shoulder.

I flexed my hands. "We better hurry, Robert."

He arched a brow my way and paused. "You've got somewhere else to be, princess? I thought I had this day with you?" He glanced at his watch then at me. "At least until five. Don't tell me you're backing out now."

I chuckled while retrieving our selections from his basket and placing them onto the produce belt for self-checkout at the register. "No, I'm not bailing on you if that's what you mean. Remember the flyer we saw yesterday at the hotel lounge? There'll be a special exhibit at the museum at noon today, and we'd agreed to go see it. It's ten thirty now, and we're making a stop at the hospital to see Detective Mike first."

He exhaled, grabbing the produce as I bagged it. "Oh, I'm sorry! I did forget. In that case, you go ahead. I'll grab the bags. I'm right behind you." From then on, there was a noticeable pep in his step, and he wore his enthusiasm literally on his sleeves.

~

We hurried along and were able to arrive at the hospital around eleven. The strong odor of a disinfectant substance filled the ICU hallway when we entered, and Robert stepped in first into Detective Mike's room.

I followed him with a bag of the produce we'd purchased as gifts. When I looked around. There were wires everywhere, and they had multiple colors and were all connected to different parts of him. I swallowed hard, trying to maintain composure, but all I could see in my mind's eye was a reflection of the multi-wire machine at Cortexe Corp. My hands began to shake, even as I drew closer to the bed, at Robert's beckon.

Detective Mike's face looked worn out, his eyes were drawn and puffy as he turned toward the sound of our entry, and both of his arms were fully bandaged. He gave a wan smile. "You're Ruby, aren't you? I'm glad you made it out of Cortexe Corp.," he said with a soft but strained voice, although his eyes were sharp as he looked straight at me.

I nodded. Robert had mentioned that Mike was out when the choppers had arrived at Cortexe Corp. "Thank you." I pointed to his arm. "I'm relieved to see you in better shape. I'm sure you'll be up and kicking in no time at all." That was all I could manage. I couldn't take it any longer as my belly now churned intensely. I was breaking out in cold sweats, and panic was rising rapidly inside me as the wires blurred in my eyes and the memory of captivity persisted.

I could mentally picture Pete Zendel's face and his brown eyes covered by his dark glasses, laughing with the cube in hand—all in my mind's eye. Sure, it wasn't real, but the memory got to me nevertheless. I felt bad about leaving the room, but I had to go or else I could pass out. As much as I cared about Robert's friend and his recovery, I didn't want to become a medical emergency either. So I took a couple of steps backward toward the door. "Robert, I'll leave you two alone to catch up. I'll be right outside." I fled the room before he had a chance to ask me why.

Out in the hallway, I give a cursory smile at a nurse who walked past me, but whom I barely saw through dizzying eyes while trying hard to appear calm and collected. I opened my mouth and gulped in deep breaths. Then I leaned my shoulders against the wall for support.

Soon, Robert came out and grabbed the bag of fruit I'd set down beside me, and then he hurried back into the room. Minutes later, he returned at a more leisurely pace.

I was still leaning on the wall, although I'd straightened my posture a bit when he approached. "What is going on, Ruby? Are you all right? You literally ran out of there." A crease formed on his forehead as his eyes searched my face.

I winced at the concern I must've caused them. "I'm very sorry if I offended your friend, but I couldn't be in there any longer. I couldn't take it anymore. Not with all those wires...they reminded me of The New Rulebook machine and of Pete Zendel. It felt like I was reliving the trauma all over again. I know it wasn't real, but the memory was just as potent. I'm so sorry."

He took my hand and squeezed it gently. Then he drew me into a warm embrace. "I'm truly sorry, Ruby. It's my fault because I should have warned you before we went inside."

I shook my head, cradled on his chest, although he couldn't see it. "No, it's not your fault. There was no way you could've known, because you weren't there." Sudden warmth spread over me like a sheet, and heat rose to my cheeks. Suddenly, I wanted to hold him tighter and closer so I stepped back, yanking my hands free of him.

As a distraction, I turned my focus toward the other end of the hallway, out of his line of sight. I real-

ized that I couldn't keep up the pretense that I didn't
feel anything for him when my feelings kept growing
stronger by the day. But again, what was I supposed to
do with them? For starters, I needed these seven days
I was about to spend with Robert as much as he did to
reconnect and to help him get back to his feet. Then
I'd have to create some distance—for his sake and
mine.

It had been three days since Robert and I began
to spend more time together. It was the fourth
day now, which had been mostly emotional-
event free for me, to my relief. We'd spent the second
and third days at an open park near the hotel, grabbing lunch from passing food trucks, and then we
patronized hot dog stands for snacks. We'd also had
great conversations as we talked about people from
the past that we missed and would like to see again,
about new friends we'd made, including the hotel
owner, Mr. Samuels, who'd offered us free morning
tea and coffee. Then our chat veered off into people
who we wished we could forget, like those who made
high school unbearable, and finally his little friends
from the orphanage whom he told me were now in
college and were doing well.

Before we knew it, the time was already five in the
evening. We grabbed takeout at a sub restaurant then
returned to the hotel. Thankfully, the MPD kept our
location a secret since we left the Windstar building

two days ago, after giving oral and written eyewitness accounts of our experiences. Out of the blue, the MPD had bestowed honorary awards to Robert, Detective Mike, and me. Robert was submitted for another promotion, and the members of the Special Investigations' unit were honored as a group for their efforts against The New Rulebook.

The government launched an investigation into all Cortexe Corp.'s activities to assess how much damage The New Rulebook may have already done. We only gave a few press interviews, and we rather referred others to the MPD regarding any comments on The New Rulebook and Pete Zendel, who had been nicknamed by the public as "the evil twin". Obviously, he was a nightmare no one wanted to relive again by repeatedly talking about him. Violet Zendel, on the other hand, received a posthumous award for her bravery and for her role in assisting the MPD.

I was inducted into the Police Honor Society— though I was not sure what I was supposed to do there—and I was promised a ticket to their annual dinner during Christmas. Robert was nominated to chair a panel on plotting the way forward for protective global security interactions. He also received awards for bravery and courage.

Since that day, I saw the light returning to his face, and his eyes regained their usual sparkle. I pondered on what our time together was achieving, at least for me, knowing it was much more than just whiling away time. I didn't want to waste it. Instead, I wanted to invest it productively. For one, going out every day

had kept me from thinking about my captivity experience at Cortexe Corp. It had given me the assurance
that there was something sweet about ordinary daily
life, that I'd previously missed. Now, thankfully, I had
a rare opportunity to spend quality time with Robert
—someone dear to me whom I'd thought was dead.

I rose and parted the blinds. Then I looked out the
window at the view. The dark blanket of the skies
above melded with the bright city lights below.
Moments later, I let the curtain fall and walked over to
the closet. Over on the wall, the clock said it was
eleven o'clock. *Definitely past the time I should be
sleeping to get an early start tomorrow.* Pulling a white
drawer open, I selected a sky-blue colored top and
bottom matching pair of pajamas, and I slipped into
them as a yawn escaped my lips.

I realized again just then how close I'd been to
losing Robert for good. I could hardly imagine that we
got a second chance at life—which only a few people
in such situations typically did—especially considering that we didn't part on good terms at the time,
with him being saved and me not yet saved. This time,
however, I intentionally chose to maximize the value
of each moment we spent together every day, to be
fully aware of every passing moment, and to treasure
them.

I walked over to the bed, then pulled aside the
huge comforters. Slipping off my shoes, I climbed into
bed and reached for the bedside lamp to switch it off,
but first, I picked up my Bible instead to read a verse
before turning in for the night.

I ruminated with a smile at a verse in the book of Psalms just as the phone rang. I wondered who could be calling me this late at night? But I placed my Bible down, and I picked up the receiver. "Hello?"

"It's me. Robert. I'm simply checking on you to be sure that you're okay."

My shoulders slacked, and I exhaled in relief. "Oh, okay, I was wondering who it was."

He cleared his throat and asked. "Is your room comfortable enough?" I heard him tap the phone's speaker at his end, probably to make sure he could hear me well. This was the first time he'd asked me about my room, maybe because we'd been busy catching up on the past and had not discussed enough about the present and the future.

I scanned my plush accommodations and chuckled. "Yes, it's pretty decent. How about yours?"

He laughed and static crackled. "Me? Oh, I could sleep on a couch for all I care. The king-size bed I've got here is not bad. Not bad at all."

I rubbed my neck. "It really feels different, Robert. Now, I can put my feet down to the carpet without worrying about lasers chomping my toes off. I can't believe how much I now appreciate the littlest things—"

"Starting with oxygen," he cut in, like he used to, and that warmed my heart. I knew why he appreciated the air most. I recalled his choking experience on the Cortexe Corp. COO's cigar. It was tough to watch, and it must've been tougher to experience. It was funny how I didn't remember seeing the COO in the room when The New Rulebook launched—even all of his enthusiasm didn't get him into the room when it mattered most.

"Red, do this for me now, if you'd please. Plant your feet solidly on the ground. Then say something you feel like you haven't been able to thank God for."

"Sounds like a good plan." Then I remembered I'd recently had trouble stepping from a bed to the ground. It had tortured me for days, and I suspected Robert may have noticed this on the only occasion I entered his room—the night of the awards—and excitedly dove onto the bed when I spotted a box of dark chocolate on it. I'd sat there and ate up happily. Until he took his shirt off while changing from the uniform worn for the day ceremony, to a suit for the dinner party, standing by the dresser, right there, I was eager to leave just as quickly as I'd entered.

The problem was that I had to get down from the bed first, which meant planting my feet on the ground. I sat up, but I couldn't go beyond that. Then I panicked. The Cortexe Corp. memory came flooding in like rushing water. I wasn't sure how much time had passed after which Robert came close and took my hand. Smiling, he'd pulled me to my feet. He didn't say a word, neither did I. I simply left.

I'd hoped the horror would go away on its own, but sadly, it hadn't. But I could break free of the hold of these memories. *Now.* "Okay. Please stay with me on the phone."

I threw back the covers and swung my legs low, and they got close to the ground but not quite there.

Then I was afraid to move any farther. The flap of curtains to steady air from the overhead vent momentarily distracted me, but I swallowed and refocused again. I had to do this. My indoor shoes, although close by, felt miles out of reach. My heart beat faster as I pressed my hands on both sides of the bed, sliding outward. My feet neared the spot where those laser beams were set at Cortexe Corp., and I instinctively stopped.

My neck muscles felt taut against my shoulders like stretched strings on a guitar. My eyes were shut tightly, and I ground my teeth involuntarily. I didn't know it would be this hard. But I had to conquer the memory, *every* bad memory of my terrible experience at Cortexe Corp.

Dear Jesus, please help me. I can't help myself. You said You will never leave me nor forsake me. Like a life-giving waterfall, strength of heart from nowhere filled me, and I pushed my feet closer to the lime-colored carpet.

"You got it, Red. One step, and you've overcome. He can't hurt you now." Robert's voice gave me so much courage—and support.

Dear Jesus, I know You have a solid hand underneath my feet. I breathed in deeply again, gripping the bedside tighter, as I felt a persistent edge of courage coming on me again.

"Get Pete Zendel out of your head, Red! You can do this," Robert shouted from the phone I'd placed on speaker.

I tapped my feet on the ground without thinking

about it as his words spurred me on. Then I rose to full height and took another step along the edge of the bed. Then another. Until I was walking around those edges where the laser beam would have been. Triumphant, I jumped for joy.

"Yessss! I did it! I'm free. Thank You, Jesus." My ecstasy knew no bounds, my hands flew free in the air, and my feet jumped high. Tears of gratitude welling from my newfound freedom rolled down my cheeks. I no longer felt an accelerated heartbeat, just my normal self. Then I made a snap decision. I picked up the phone to convey it to Robert and removed our call from speaker.

"Robert?"

"Yes?" he answered, excitement clear in his voice, and my heart thrilled to hear him so happy for me.

I exhaled, gripping the phone a little tighter, with the mouthpiece edged closer to my ear. My decision felt clearly written in the smiles spreading all over my face. "We're going back to the hospital first thing tomorrow morning. I'm going to conquer those wires."

He laughed out loud with lightness lacing his voice. "If you say so, Ruby. If you say so. Goodnight and huge congratulations!"

The following morning, we entered Mercy Memorial Hospital again around eleven. This time, I was leading Robert in. The disinfectant smell of the intensive care unit's hallway now felt familiar, even less alien. We approached Detective Mike's room, and I freed my arms, dangling my purse by its zipper ring, brimming with the determination to walk in free and walk out free. The nursing staff, upon recognizing us, smiled, then waved us through.

I stopped at the door and turned to Robert so he nodded for me to go in first. That emboldened me, and as I squeezed the doorknob, it felt as though I'd stopped breathing for a moment. Then I strode purposefully forward. No one else would understand what was going on except Robert and me, not even Detective Mike. I pushed the doors wide open, stepped into the well-lit room, and in my face, stared the same set of wires, but they somehow appeared to be more aggressive to my mind today. Defying their threatening dangles, I strutted to the middle of the room. After taking in a deep breath, I pressed my eyes shut.

Robert's reassuring hand came up softly on my back. "You can do this. I know you can," he whispered, and his gentle voice prodded me forward. I heard the constant beeps from the monitors, but instead of them giving me a scare like before, they only fueled me with more courage. I took in another deep breath as I exhaled. *Thank You, Jesus, because You said that,*

whoever You've set free is free indeed. You've set me free.
Therefore, I receive my freedom in You. I opened my eyes
as sudden faith welled up in the depth of my being,
spreading like wildfire inside me and urged me
forward. I chose in that very moment to see through
eyes of faith and no longer by how I felt. I approached
the bed, and I tapped one of the wires lightly. It felt
tender beneath my fingers and suddenly nonthreaten-
ing. That was it. I had won, yet again, and I was truly
free.

"Hello, beautiful. Good to see you again. Hope
you're not in a hurry this time." I swung around at the
sound of his voice and saw the detective grinning.

Then, seeing I was much calmer that the last time
we were here, Robert stepped forward and laid a
supportive hand on my arm. "No, she's here to get to
know you better, buddy. And to hear how much you
said you suck at predicting football wins."

We all broke out in laughter, and the tension
vanished from the room.

Robert took a spot near the center of the bed,
sitting closer to Detective Mike while I perched on the
other end near his feet. There were empty chairs, but
proximity mattered more to us right now. We sat and
talked for over an hour just as the wires and their
threat faded out of my mind forever.

～

The last two days of our time together passed quickly. We visited neighboring restaurants and sampled a variety of international dishes. Five restaurants captured our interest the most. We enjoyed crispy South American tacos at the Regano Eatery—which was our first stop. The Royale African restaurant served us delicious jollof rice with stewed chicken and seasoned with spicy hot pepper for lunch. Next, we opted for Hidden Desert—a Middle Eastern eatery—where original hummus served with fresh-baked bread welcomed us for dinner. On the following day, we visited Ria Garden-Style Italian for homemade-style, all-natural ingredient pizza paired with white Parisian wine. For lunch, we enjoyed spicy jerk chicken and curry goat at The Lasalle Caribbean restaurant. Then we ate rare American tossed salad with grilled salmon sprinkled with salt-free herbs for dinner at The Wooden Roast. They were all deliciously satisfying, though Robert had to gulp down lots of water after the first spoonful of each spicy meal—then he stubbornly ate it all up, smacking his lips at the end.

Laughter filled our experiences, but I felt like I was beginning to have too much fun. There were still...issues...to sort out, but I didn't have the right answers yet. So I decided to talk to Jesus about Robert first before talking to Robert about us. For now, the joys of exploration were sufficient.

14

THERE ARE MANY DEVICES IN A MAN'S HEART; BUT THE counsel of the Lord, that shall stand. -Proverbs 19:21

"Ms. Ruby, do you want more coffee?"

Becky, a service attendant, set an extra cup of fresh brew on my table. She had been serving me free coffee, and Robert free tea, since our arrival, courtesy of Mr. Samuels, the hotel owner.

"Thank you, Becky, you are very kind. This should be my last cup for now."

She smiled, and then took the earlier emptied cup, setting down a mug of fresh milk and some sweetener for my next round.

My phone vibrated, bringing my attention back to the résumés stacked in front of me. Three weeks had gone by since Robert and I spent some time together. And although I'd enjoyed every moment, I quickly got back into the swing of daily living while Robert returned to duty at the MPD. I started rebuilding my delivery business, nearly from scratch.

With our current near-celebrity status, the influx of new clients had become overwhelming. I reestablished contact with my previous clients, arranging to resume services for them, again, especially focusing first on securing my service for the seniors. They were very glad to have me back and safe, especially Ms. Bryant. At such growth rate, I thought of going downtown to rent some office space on my own. However, Robert had insisted that I waited another month until my birthday for his "surprise" birthday gift—referring to the house where he'd sheltered me while fleeing Cortexe Corp. He'd said he was finalizing things like furniture and other minor details. Since I'd hated to ruin his good intentions, I chose to wait, now temporarily running my business from my hotel room.

I looked up to see Tony, our evening steward striding past me. "Hello, Tony."

"Hi, Ms. Ruby." He waved to me, flashing me a broad smile. Tony served visitors on my floor evening snacks. Based on my request, he'd faithfully delivered a cup of blended frozen watermelon slush every night to my room, leaving it set by the door. At nine, I usually poked my head out and snatched it up from the tray. I would snack on it while working late most nights or just before bed. Its sweetness and natural flavor helped me to be well rested and ready to rise every morning with a clear head and a winning attitude.

"Ma'am, the car's ready. We can leave whenever you'd like us to," Chancy, my driver, chimed from the lobby entrance. He was a gregarious fellow with a lovely wife and two beautiful kids, who were five and nine years old, respectively.

I waved my full palm, pleading for his patience. "Five more minutes, Chancy. I'll be right there." I paid him daily for his services in taking me around town in a rental car since, for safety's sake, the police were still checking out my car and apartment.

He was driving me downtown to the MPD so I could interview candidates who'd applied to be my delivery assistants. They would assist me with making deliveries all across town due to increased business demands. Robert had suggested it to reduce risking my safety. However, I still handled select deliveries for top well-known clients.

I flipped to a passage in my Bible, reading a snippet before heading out for the day. I was tremendously grateful to spot a pocket-sized, free New Testament Bible, perched by my bedside lamp on my first night at the hotel. Raw from my traumatic experience, and hungry from receiving Jesus in captivity, I'd devoured the book of Matthew on the first night before getting a three-hour shut-eye right close to daybreak. It had been one of my first pleasures of the day, every day since.

After reading a short passage now, I rose, taking my new laptop and sliding it into a backpack. Robert had also installed every possible antivirus, antimalware, and tamper-proof protection on it, and I'd let him know that I felt most secure. We purchased new mobile phones, disabling everything except the call, text, and email features. I'd argued for us to get contemporary phones and disable anything we didn't want, rather than go back to Stone Age communications. At the time, Robert reluctantly agreed. Now, he was the one who couldn't stop turning on one feature after the other on our phones, testing them out, and announcing how amazing they were.

I smiled at the memory while exiting the hotel lobby to the entrance, searching for where Chancy was waiting with the vehicle so I could walk over to him. Tooting horns sounded close by, drawing my attention to my left.

Chancy drove and rounded the bend into the parking lot, stopping right in front of me.

I entered the vehicle, placing my purse beside me on the seat. My new charm bracelet came into view as I bit into an apple I'd packed for a quick, on-the-go breakfast. Symbols representing red for love, white for faith, clear for hope, as well as a gray cross, all dangled from the bracelet. We'd been gifted one bracelet each when Robert and I had worshiped at the New Life Assembly the first time three Sundays ago. He'd been on duty every Sunday since so I attended alone these days. We went there after searching and asking around for a good Christian gathering where

Christ Jesus and the true Word of God was preached.
Out of several recommendations, we'd prayed. Then
we decided to try New Life first. It was close to the
hotel too. Both the warmth with which we were
received and the sound Bible-based message
preached by the pastor sealed our choice.

Robert and I had little face-to-face interaction in
recent weeks due to our busy schedules. We texted
once daily by mutual agreement, to check in with
each other. But most of the new distance was my fault.
I'd needed physical space from Robert. He hadn't
been central to my thoughts since, although he still
lingered in the background. With my business picking
up speed, it was probably time to speak to God in
prayer about Robert.

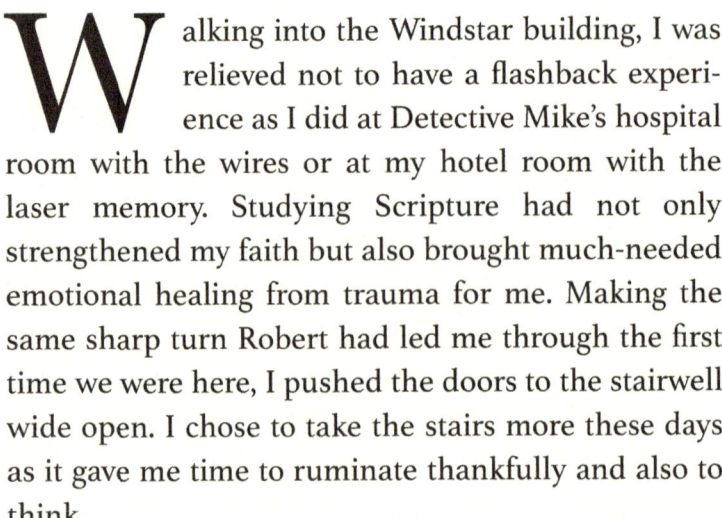

Walking into the Windstar building, I was
relieved not to have a flashback experience as I did at Detective Mike's hospital
room with the wires or at my hotel room with the
laser memory. Studying Scripture had not only
strengthened my faith but also brought much-needed
emotional healing from trauma for me. Making the
same sharp turn Robert had led me through the first
time we were here, I pushed the doors to the stairwell
wide open. I chose to take the stairs more these days
as it gave me time to ruminate thankfully and also to
think.

As I emerged at the entrance to the MPD, an

officer greeted me upon arrival and led me to a conference room while my interviewees sat in a waiting area just outside of it. He informed me that Robert was out in the field, which was fine by me. When we rounded a bend to the conference room area, another officer threw up his hands in the air. "The system is down." A few more officers grunted in affirmation from their desks.

We entered the conference room, and the officer, who'd escorted me in, left. I was thankful that the MPD had provided me with their conference room for a one-hour use today out of courtesy since technically my home office was under police occupation. Though I was not an officer, however, I was presently viewed as a friend to law enforcement, thanks to The New Rulebook's takedown. I was grateful for the offer because I was ready to interview candidates standing under a tree if need be. I set down my purse on an adjoining seat and settled into a chair at the center of the room for the interview, praying inwardly for divine direction. I rose, strode to the door, and welcomed my first of ten candidates, intent on choosing five out of them all as finalists.

The interviews happened quickly and having read the résumés beforehand, I'd whittled down the ten candidates from a long list. This was more an effort to obtain the reasons for their interest in the job and to see if they were good fits.

Their personalities shone through each interview, and I knew it would be tough making five selections because each person seemed great on their own merit. Except I couldn't afford to hire all of them.

When the interviews were over, Alyssa, Catherine, Vin, Kwame, and Destine were my final choices. Alyssa, Vin, and Kwame were fresh high-school graduates while Destine and Catherine were college freshmen studying Business Marketing. I felt as though I'd chosen a good team, who were goal-driven and well able to support my business. I shook hands with my final-choice candidates, promising to make them formal offers of employment by the end of the week. Meanwhile, I made a mental note to run their background checks with the MPD, and then sort out their paperwork before making any offers. It was too bad that the system was currently down.

Some minutes after the interviewees left, I exited the conference room, satisfied, and searched for the officer who'd escorted me in.

"Hey, there. I heard you were around, so I was coming to see you." I knew it was Robert, and even though I hadn't heard his voice in a while, I was amazed at how I reacted the same way inside—butterflies in my stomach.

I took a moment to gather my nerves before turning. "Yes, we just wrapped up. It's good to see you."

His brows arched, and a smile crossed his face briefly. "Whoa. You don't seem excited. Did everything go well with the candidates or did someone perform poorly?"

How did I ever think he wouldn't notice my guarded attitude? So I clutched my purse tighter and tried to sound even. "Actually, it went great, and I selected five outstanding candidates. If their background checks come back clean, I'm making them offers by the end of this week."

His eyes traveled all the way down to my feet, then back up to my face, and lingered. "You look good. I presume you've been resting well."

Heat rose speedily to my cheeks, but I stemmed it pretty fast. *Maybe he's truly paying me an innocent compliment.* I chided myself not to read something into everything he did. I rubbed my neck and looked away. "I slept as much as I can, although it's been quite busy."

He agreed with a nod. "I know, you can say that again, as it's been the same with me here. Matter of fact, it's been tough out there, too, on the streets, but I'm glad to be back to protecting." He pointed toward the door. "Want to grab an early lunch with this old friend?"

I smiled, just realizing then I hadn't eaten anything yet. "Sure. I'm starving anyway. Wait, I need to thank someone first." I spotted the officer who'd led me in and strode purposefully toward him.

～

"Which meal tickles your fancy, madam?" Robert playfully said as he accepted lunch menu cards from the waiter serving our table.

Inviting aromas from the food served at the nearby tables made my stomach growl. I browsed the information while glad the lunch menu at The Grille Garden had tempting spring season specials being offered today.

Pasta dipped in white wine, sprinkled with garlic-seasoned herbs, and served with a side of fresh strawberries, sounded appetizing and already made my mouth water. A dot of one leaf of spinach twisted with a slice of lemon, cleaved onto the side of our water glasses. I was happy to see that the meal came with a tossed salad to-go.

"I'll go with meal number three, the pasta meal." Having made my choice, I handed the menu back to the waiter.

Robert peered at his menu closely as though searching for my choice. Then he smiled, confirming my suspicion. "Now eating greens, huh? Good. I told you back at the orphanage that you'd join me one day." A teasing smile lit up the corner of his eyes.

I shrugged, downplaying my choice, though it was a big step for me. "I'm learning to like them, though I'm not a sworn fan of green foods yet."

He then handed his menu back to the waiter. "I'll have what the smart lady's having. Plus, make it diced apples for a side."

I glanced up sharply, surprised. He knew I liked apples so he must've ordered those for me. "Robert, you didn't have to."

He waved it off. "I know you love apples, plus I figured you might have needed something to brighten your day."

I looked away quickly as I'd tried hard to appear cheerful during our trip to the restaurant. But these regenerated feelings had left me feeling like a full drum was sitting on my mind. I was still in love with Robert Towers. And the distance had only made it grow stronger. I pressed my lips together and tried to navigate a way out of the current topic of conversation.

Just then, Robert rose and walked over to me, grabbing a close-by seat from an empty table and setting it down right next to me. He gazed uninterrupted into my eyes. Then he spoke softly, "Red, I hate seeing you like this. Something is eating away at you. I can see that clearly. Now, do you want to tell me or am I going to have to prod it out of you? You choose."

I looked into his green depths and wondered, will I ever not love them the way I do right now? Do I just tell him what I feel and be done with it? "I—"

"Ma'am, here's your order. The fresh-baked bread is on the house. Bon appétit." Our waiter smiled cheerfully, setting my meal down and interrupting our conversation.

"Oh thanks. Let's eat already!" I concurred, eager to divert the attention from me.

The waiter gathered our empty water glasses and

refilled them, and then he walked to a point nearby, waiting on us.

My exclamation succeeded in setting Robert on his feet and back to his seat at our table. He grew quiet as our forks and spoons did the talking for the next half hour. I was afraid he might have seen too much in my eyes earlier. But I chose not to say anything further. Seriously, it was time to take this matter to the only One who could sort this out well—for everyone's good.

15

A WORTHY WOMAN WHO CAN FIND? FOR HER PRICE IS FAR above rubies. -Proverbs 31:10 [ASV]

A phone ringing loudly yanked me out of troubled sleep. My hands scrambled frantically, searching for the receiver. Finally, I grasped its cold solid and placed it against my ear.

"Hello?" I sounded groggy even to myself, and I still felt awfully tired too.

"Ms. Ruby, would you like me to remove the watermelon serve still sitting in front of your room?"

Oh goodness. I was so engrossed last night that I'd forgotten to take my watermelon slush! "I'm so sorry, Tony. I completely forgot. Yes, please. You can take it away. Thank you." I put down the receiver, my fingers flash-combing through my roughened hair. I'd even forgotten to put my hair in a bun before sleeping. I wasn't looking forward to the tough task of combing through it this morning. However, I wouldn't blame myself too much since I'd had a rather busy night.

After returning to the hotel, I spent all night praying for divine guidance about Robert. I poured out my heart to Jesus, telling Him how I felt—how I really felt inside about Robert. I lined out the pros and cons of either choice I could make. I waited to hear Him as before at Cortexe Corp.—a sure voice inside—but I'd heard nothing. I got tired around four in the morning and retired, falling asleep right away.

I rose to my feet, and I twisted the small desk clock around to reveal the time—7:35 a.m. Stretching to release the kinks in my muscles, I made my way to the bathroom but stepped back briefly to read Scripture and thank God for a new, blessed day, as was now my practice. I lifted up my small Bible resting on the side desk beside a lamp and turned to where I'd markedly stopped the previous day. Then I read how Peter fished all night but caught nothing. Then how Jesus came to him in the morning and Peter ended up with his boat being filled to overflowing with fish.

I closed my Bible, thinking for a moment how much Peter and I had in common right now. I'd prayed all night but got nothing. The thought made me chuckle as I placed the Bible back on the desk. Today, I'd gotten a new day and a full afternoon schedule to look forward to. Since my Cortexe Corp. experience, I had decided to start every day with a huge smile and with joy in my heart—no matter what.

With that thought and a big smile ear to ear, I headed to the bathroom for a hot, refreshing shower.

～

"**D**o you want your usual?" Becky asked while placing clean drinking water cups on a shelf.

I smiled, feeling grateful that she'd remembered my preference every morning. I chose to sit near the window beside the fresh green flowers set in vases on its ledge. "Yes, please. Thank you very much."

I came down for coffee, dressed in a sleeveless shirt and shorts, without my usual baggage of work materials because I had a tough night. So today, I just wanted to breathe in the fresh air first, then take a break this morning, and return my attention to handling my business matters in the afternoon.

The sun rose steadily over the horizon, yielding a crisp, clear view from where I sat. I savored the warmth of the sunshine on my skin and drew in a deep breath of clean air, thankful for this time alone. White lace curtains fluttered as cool air blew in softly. A stray sunflower, still set in its stem, laid lazily on the slightly open windowsill. I took in the relaxed, calming view.

"Good morning, Red. Are you watching the sun rise?" Robert beamed as he strode toward me from across the room. Strolling leisurely, he was clad in dark blue jeans and an orange shirt. "Did you sleep well?" he asked, arriving at my table.

A nervous smile crossed my face briefly as I wondered how he'd react if he knew I'd barely slept—because of *him*.

"You know..." I trailed off as he pulled back the opposite chair and took a seat. "What about you? Did you sleep well?" I watched him answer from beyond the rim of my coffee cup.

Nodding toward Becky, he signaled her for his usual tea. "It was more the same as usual. I had worked until the wee hours of the morning today, but I can't complain, though, since it was necessary that I get some stuff done."

Becky served him his tea, and hot steam rose high from his cup, blending in lazily into the air.

I focused on sipping mine. "Thank you very much, Becky."

She nodded an acknowledgment. Then she grinned and walked away.

I raised my head to find him staring at me and smiling warmly. Caught, he looked up skyward and out the window. Then he laughed, and his gaze returned to me with the same fervency as before. "This rising sun, beautiful as it looks, dwarfs in comparison to how beautiful you are inside and out." He pressed his lips tightly, as though struggling to hold back more things he could say. Just then, a fountain of urgency welled up deep inside me, simmering just above the surface. He stood, closing the short distance to the window with two strong strides, with his hands slid into his pockets. Brilliant rays of sunlight showered him with a natural glow.

"I thank God for this beautiful sunrise! But I thank God more for you," Robert exclaimed. "Red, you need to see this from where I stand."

Smiling, I looked up at him, and I thought, no, he needed to see what was going on from where I sat! Those rays of sunlight formed a glorious glow around him, highlighting his sharp features, making them finer. I gasped as peace flooded my soul, all of a sudden, and then I knew that I'd gotten my answer. He was never meant to only be my best friend. Rather, he was always meant by God to be my soul mate.

"When I see such radiance on your face, I know something good is going on behind those eyes. Do you want to share?" His breath blew softly close to my ears. Then he turned, stepping into full view as his eyes gleamed, full of admiration for me.

I was so enraptured by the conviction I felt that I didn't see him come up close, but I knew it was now time to open up to him about how I felt about him. It wasn't easy opening yourself up to possible hurt, but I was going to take this leap of faith unafraid of where it led. I smiled, placing a gentle hand on his arm. "Robert, what if I told you I've been in love with you since we reunited at the chopper?" I waited with bated breath, not sure what was coming. Did Robert still love me or had I waited too late to return his love? Either way, I would simply trust God and move forward.

He was quiet for a while. Then he glanced up at me with glassy eyes. "I'd say that is incredible, and then ask why on earth it took you this long to tell me?

I've been dying in silence all this time, wondering how long I've got to endure how I feel about you before having to let you go."

I blinked, and I could hardly believe my ears. Gratitude to God welled up inside me, and we held each other's hands, feeling nothing but peace around us. Everything and everyone faded into the background. Only Robert and I were left in this universe of love and quiet acceptance of God's perfect will. Our hearts radiated with love as strong as the rays of sunlight shining upon us both at such perfect timing. With everything we'd been through, there could be no sweeter ending than finding this God-led love with each other. God did make all things beautiful at His time, as Scripture says. His time was truly the best.

Then to my surprise, Robert went down on one knee, so I gasped and blinked even harder to be sure I was seeing correctly.

A few gasps echoed around us as well while my hands flew to my mouth. *What was he doing?*

But Robert was on a roll as he dipped his hand into his pocket, pulled out a small gray box with silver-finished edges. "Red, I've been carrying this around for two weeks, waiting for the right time to ask you. You hadn't wanted an intimate relationship with me before, but that was before Cortexe Corp. Before our brutal experiences at the hands of Pete Zendel." He released a small latch on the box, and more gasps trailed his action. Looking up, his green emeralds firmly locked on my brown ones. "That was before you wouldn't let me hold your hand for over a minute without snatching yours back, and before you refused to let me rub your tense shoulders, which never bothered you before, and when you looked away whenever my shirt came off—yeah, I noticed."

Heat spread to my embarrassed cheeks, but I wanted to hear all that he had to say. This was our moment.

"I knew something had changed, and I knew you now had feelings for me which you were struggling to accept. So, I gave you room to sort it out." Tears streamed down both of our faces. Then he reached out and wiped mine away, but he was a bit late, for a couple of stray tears had already dropped.

I wiped his tears too, intent to make sure he would never shed tears for me out of pain again, if I could help it. "Why didn't you just...let me go when I didn't say anything to you?" I asked with a choked voice.

He shut his eyes momentarily. Then he lifted my hand, planting a firm kiss on my wrist. "I couldn't, I just wouldn't. What we had was special, and I knew it was God-ordained so I had to wait you out. And it was hard." He chuckled as he shook his head, and his thick brown curls bounced from side to side. "I had to fight—for you. You were worth the wait, so I couldn't give up just yet—unless you asked me to. Which you hadn't."

His words were hitting every point of doubt I still had and readily knocking them all off until the only thing left was peace. We had so much to figure out, so much to learn, about Jesus, about our new faith, and we could joyfully look forward to our new future. But he had to know why I wasn't forthcoming at first, why I had been silent. "Robert, I didn't tell you first because I wanted you to be happy. I wanted to step aside so you could find someone else if the person would make you happy. I didn't want to obstruct your happiness by taking advantage of our proximity." I pressed my lips together while a fresh wave of joy washed over me. "I also had to ask my best friend first."

Confusion dipped his brows. "You mean, ask me?"

I threw my head back a little, and a small laugh escaped. "No, not you. My new best friend, Jesus. I talk to Him about everything, and everyone, since that laser-room encounter at Cortexe Corp.—and everyone includes you. I needed to be sure about us. Now, I am."

His Adam's apple bobbed as he chuckled softly. "Ruby, when we were kidnapped, I didn't ask you to call on Jesus because you were weak." His voice thickened with emotion. "That was what I was trying to communicate to you when the glass was broken at your apartment. I wanted to share Christ with you, but I guess it wasn't the right time. Divine timing is the best, and it always is. As I inferred earlier, Ruby, you're the strongest person I know, so you're not weak —sometimes, you're even stronger at heart than I am. I see you rise against the odds every day and never wait for a handout from anyone. But after my salvation experience, I knew deep inside me that your strength would not be sufficient at some point. When the storms of life come, you'd need someone stronger than you or me—than any human being—to hold you when no one else can, and I'm so happy you yielded to Him! It's the best experience anyone can encounter, because it's life changing for good."

I realized then that a crowd of well-wishers had formed around us, and an elderly man walking with a cane drew closer and leaned forward toward Robert. "Ask her already, young man. Women aren't patient in this sort of thing."

Laughter and cheers broke out in the crowd as Robert smiled and brought down his second knee, now kneeling on both legs. He took my hand, and I rose to my feet, feeling awestruck. He then opened the box in his hand, and a beautiful ring, cast in exquisite pink sapphires shone brightly, helped by the sunlight. "This is the only thing I have left from my parents. It was my grandmother's. Ruby Masters, would you make me the happiest man on earth by marrying me? I love you so much, and I want to spend the rest of my life loving you, serving you, protecting you, and making you laugh. Please marry me, Red."

Tears still rolled down my cheeks while my heart bubbled with joy. I nodded, and then I laughed. "Yes, Robert Towers. I'll marry you, Emerald Eyes."

He slipped the ring onto my left ring finger, then stood and hugged me tightly. Applause broke out across the room. But he was squeezing precious air out of my lungs so I pressed him back slightly. "Robert, I need some air."

At the realization, he pulled back a little but didn't let me go as he whispered, "I'm sorry."

I smiled and tugged at his shirt. "You're holding me like I'm going to fly away."

He laughed and embraced me again, inhaling my scent. "Don't blame me, Red. I'm a man fighting for the love of his heart, like vanilla fighting for chocolate."

He interlocked his left fingers with mine, and the deal was sealed.

And just like Peter in Scripture, God gave me a net-breaking miracle in the morning!

With an eager heart, I looked forward to our future together.

Robert's phone rang so he stood as the crowd dispersed. He answered the call, then he frowned. "Yes, sir. I understand."

He gripped my hand. "Something is going on, but I'm not sure what it is. I have to get to the station." He relaxed his grip and peered in my face. "Will you be all right here?"

A quick nod followed. "Yes. I'll be fine."

He shifted to walk toward the stairs. "Okay. I'll go get dressed and head down there. It might be urgent since the captain called me himself. I don't want to keep him waiting."

I sucked in my lip and felt my brows dip. "Be careful. God will keep you safe."

His face relaxed a little. "I will. Thank you."

As he spun to leave, my chest tightened. *Lord Jesus, please protect Robert for me—everyday.* That was all I could do right now.

But only God could see what had targeted them

for destruction in a matter of days—something cunning, dangerous and unexpected —and it wasn't even human.

***

Elsewhere in Maryland...

The Snowy Peaks Mayor Tom Barnesworth rounded a bend at the top floor of the Snowy Peaks Community Hospital—the last safe place with working comms in his town—and caught a nurse by the hand. Stepping back, he loosened his grip as she winced. "Sorry, I didn't mean to hurt you. I'm just... desperate and in a hurry."

Her eyes rounded, and she began turning toward the security station.

"Oh no. I'm not a bad guy. I'm the mayor, and this is a matter of public emergency."

He drew in a deep breath, trying to slow his racing heart so he could be calm enough to calm the woman whose help he needed. "I'm searching for my sister, the hospital matron, Peggy Barnesworth." He had twenty minutes—twenty minutes before the invaders to whom he'd lost his town could pin his location down if they'd chatted with his security detail, like he suspected they would. If his security staff resisted them, they might've bought him an extra five minutes. But, he couldn't count on that. They'd sneaked him out the back door, hoping to help him escape. He reached the road leading toward the entrance to the town and found it blocked.

No exit.

No entries.

And no help.

If only he'd stopped that ceremonial online auction! The prisoner, Pete Zendel, would not have bought his town. And now, Tom will do whatever it took to stop that criminal from physically taking over.

"I'm not sure where to find her. Sorry." The nurse ducked her head and scurried away.

Just great. He probably scared her. Cold air blasted him from a partly open window, and he groaned. Who would leave a hospital window open in winter? Glancing around, he sighed.

Oh. It was a waiting room. Nevertheless, he strode along until he came to a pause at the nursing station. He checked his watch.

Fifteen more minutes.

He shrugged his coat tighter still feeling the effect of that cold blast. If only he'd had more time to grab a bigger coat! But he couldn't complain. He was glad to even be alive. He attempted a calmer introduction this time with a forced smile that felt stiff. "Hi, I'm Mayor Barnesworth. I—"

The nurse glanced up. Then her face lit, and she pointed her pen behind her. "Oh, you're Peggy's brother. Are you here to see her?"

He exhaled. Finally, some progress. "Yes. Where can I find her?"

"She was chatting with the supervisory nurse. Go around the corner and take a left then a right."

"Thank you." He could hug her. But he had twelve minutes.

Finding Peggy wasn't hard now, not when her

laughter sailed from a room down the hall. He rapped on the door.

As he entered, she took one look at him, and that cheery laughter died. Of course, his sister could see he was in trouble. "Ms. Finley, it was nice catching up with you. If you'll excuse us, I need to speak with my brother alone."

The nurse nodded at him and exited.

Peggy grasped his hand, dragged him to the corner, and peered in his face. "Tom, what's wrong?"

"Snowy Peaks has been invaded by agents of a criminal named Pete Zendel. They are armed and dangerous. They've locked down our town. I managed to get here because you have the only working comms and I need you to send an SOS message. We have about ten to fifteen minutes if my security team was able to hold them back and buy us time."

She gasped, then gathered herself together, just like her usual manner of handling tough hospital situations. He'd watched her be brave with grieving families. Now, she was being strong again for her community. "Okay. Who do I send the message to? The cops from neighboring towns? Or Feds?"

He shook his head and checked his watch. He had to get out of the hospital fast enough to cut any connections to Peggy before they captured him. He firmed his jaw. He will not leave Snowy Peaks. He will stay here. And, whatever befell Snowy Peaks, won't happen behind him.

He swore an oath to protect this town, and he won't back away now when courage and duty called.

"No. Pete Zendel can outwit those. I need the one person who beat him and sent him to prison. Send the SOS message to a lady named Ruby Masters. Make sure she gets it. She's our last hope, Peggy."

Confusion wrinkled her forehead. Then his sister gave a nod. "I trust you. So, I'll do it. I pray to God that you are right. Let's get to the next office. I saw a recorder in there once. We can use that if you're short on time. Then I'll transmit the message."

"Let's do that." *God, please, let this work. Please let this get to Ruby and let her help us.*

"Okay. Follow me." Peggy led the way out.

Tom's message *must* reach Ruby. Or else...

THE END

NOTE FROM THE AUTHOR

Oh my. This is my first published book. I still recall how hard it was for me to write this book. Tears well up in my eyes while typing this note because people told me I wouldn't make it. Others had said no one ever made it as a writer. I was surrounded by a ton of negativity. They discouraged me at every turn but the Word of God urged me forward, and pushed me through until I wrote THE END. Now, I have more thank thirty books in total and an award-winning catalogue ALL to the glory of God.

Friends, I hope you do not discount this book whether you got it for free or paid. I would not have ever given this book away for far less than it is worth without knowing it will be a real blessing to many hearts. I am offering you a genuine treasure of mine. If this isn't your kind of story, please feel free to pass and find something you really enjoy reading.

But, if it touched your heart, brought you a smile, or encouraged you in any small way, then continue with reading the rest of this series as an appreciation of the tears, hurt, faith, passion, and sacrifice that birthed this story you've read.

Also, I pray you leave this book with more hope than pain, more joy than aches, and more of God's love in your heart. Thank you for reading! Now, on to the next book. Shall we?

Blessings to you,

Joy

August 2014

SNOWY PEAKS- BOOK 2 (SAMPLE)

~

CHAPTER ONE

"*Many a man proclaims his own loyalty, but who can find a trustworthy man?*"- *Proverbs 20:6*

. . .

RUBY MASTERS

"They're coming!" Charlie Bailey shouted, his shoulders inched high, neck tilted, and eyes primed and focused on the sky above. Eagle alert, his face showed no sign of the past two days' stress. A deep healed scar ran along his jawline, ending at his shirt's collar, meeting his gray scarf there. Offset by his dark hair, trimmed short in military-style, his eyes revealed his Asian heritage. He blinked, raised a brow, and nodded in my direction, eyes still. "I hear their metal flap." He pressed his lips tight. His clean-shaven face firmed resolute. "Ready!" He ordered the other three men.

They folded their hands behind them, also lying flat on their backs like us, and slid beneath the sewer openings. "Ready," they echoed his order.

I glanced over my right shoulder, beyond a dangling strap on my bulletproof vest. Wishing for the safety I'd felt this morning riding along the lone road from the red barn where we'd hunkered overnight. Such a contrast to these darkened tunnel-like sewer entrances. Now, the fight for survival felt primal. As though anything could come at us here. *Anything.* Except we knew what was headed our way. We met it before, and it was not human in the least. If this encounter turned violent...

I tipped my head to my right, to the telecom broadcast tower hoisted above the media building we exited minutes ago, while searching for information. "Charlie, listen, maybe there's another way." My belated effort to dissuade him from attempting force, *if* the occasion arose, sounded weak. His mind was already made up. His and the other men's. Determination reflected in his firm jaw and rigid body stance— set, determined, and ready for battle. I sighed inwardly. At least I tried. *Better late than never.*

Without a doubt, this has been the longest few minutes of my life this year. Lying flat on my back in a dried sewer entrance, waiting for danger. Too young for this. Or too old—depending on how you look at it. Plus, I'm too neat-conscious to hide in a sewer. The current circumstances don't offer me a better alternative.

The pain radiating across my back, thanks to having slept in a barn, met the brute cold chilling me from under the ground. I've never had a batch of hay for a bed, instead of a mattress, until last night at the barn. We didn't expect to get busted by crickets at the Snowy Peaks' media house. Not when the news studio appeared abandoned, like everyone had fled a sudden catastrophe—in a hurry.

The place I'd actually feared we'd be discovered was at the barn where the town's major roads ended five miles off. The area being lonely, we didn't meet a soul on our way going or coming. Out of caution, we'd gone without electricity or heat all night—and shivered throughout as a result.

I closed my eyes and replayed the SOS message I'd received. I still recalled the feminine voice—clear, but rushed and trembling. "Hello. This message is for Ruby Masters, in care of Robert Towers. This is an SOS message from the mayor of Snowy Peaks. Pete Zendel has seized our town. We need your help...." I swatted a fly, wondering how it survived the cold I presently quivered in.

A burst of sewage stench tickled my nostrils and further distracted my rehearsal. The dark half-shadow of the curved, dome-shaped bridge above hid the rest of me waist down. In contrast, the sky seemed bright, lovely even. But it wasn't simply clear sky I was seeing. The crickets were up there somewhere. And they are coming for us—now.

~

Charlie turned up his nose and blinked without looking. "I'm not changing my mind, Ruby. Not even for your fiancé, Robert, loyal as I am to him. If he was here, he would've done the same."

True, he was loyal to Robert, some would think to a fault. As partners, when in a squad car, they were like brothers and watched each other's back. Charlie had reportedly gone in and defused a bomb instead of allowing Robert to. Said he was grateful Robert harbored him for three months because he had nowhere to live after he got hired off the street while his wife and son stayed with her family. A war veteran, he was known to be patriotic and focused. His jaw tilted further skyward, left hand quietly gripping his hidden weapon, which I knew was there, tucked beneath him.

The now-familiar buzz and grating metal wings blared above. The sounds drew closer. Then they burst into view and dove lower, making for us.

Cemented block pillars separated us and these sewage entrances were located far from the center of the street. I squinted when the glint off the crickets' metal wings shone into my eye. The closer they got, the more their insides sounded like mosquitoes' whine, while the silver wings ground with a noisy flap each time they swung them. Residents claimed the place was full of them. They probably doubted what they saw up there was still the sun. At least, I thought it seemed so to the homeless man, who'd cared enough to answer us before we got here. The crickets—as they were called on the street— observed Snowy Peaks from above and then reported anomalies to whomever. I seriously doubted it was directly to Zendel, not with him still in prison.

The crickets drew closer, angling further downward, leveling with our eye view. We waited, unsure about their next move. A hidden earpiece within my ear—held in place by some powerful skin adhesive —buzzed.

I prayed Robert's design of our earpieces was flawless as touted. I attempted to focus, but the grinding flutter of the crickets' false wings, and the bothersome hum of their insides, made the creatures impossible to ignore.

They flew closer, close enough for us to look into their black, rounded, lifeless eyeballs. A camera light flashed from within.

And I blinked, turned my head from its glare. Before me, also getting observed by crickets, all four men spread out horizontally. I knew Charlie well enough to know he didn't like this. The others were newer members of Robert's unit. Though I wasn't close to them, I was almost sure they hated this encounter just as much. I imagined their hearts pounding hard as mine. I assumed that being the only unarmed person, I might pass scrutiny quicker. But I couldn't be too sure with these things though. The guys might not get so lucky. If they did, once the crickets left, I'd certainly dissuade Charlie from engaging forcibly with them if we met them again. The crickets might just be monitoring things, but someone somewhere used them to watch us. That person or people were who we needed to worry about. Violent exposure was a risk too great to take especially in a hostile environment.

Will Charlie get *this*?

Within moments, my teammates' weapons clicked behind them, and I sucked in a quick breath. Despite my aversion to this dingy atmosphere, I felt a certain kinship with all of them. My heart knotted.

What were they doing?

This was planned as an observe, learn-everything-you-can mission when we left Silver Stone. Things didn't quite go as planned, but we still needed to be careful. I didn't want to lose any of them. "Charlie..." I called through gritted teeth.

He ignored me, focusing on the fake bird fluttering in his face.

They were prepared to shoot, but what if guns couldn't stop these crickets? I swallowed. If only Robert was here. He'd know how to talk them down. Tension crackled the air and intensified with every flutter of those metal things.

Lord, make these things go away. It wasn't more a prayer than a wish. I loathed them, flutter and all.

The cricket facing me swung from the side to right in my face. Its eyes, large as tennis balls, spun around in its sockets then stopped. Its nose doubled as a beak with a flat blue tip.

I held my breath and clenched my fist as it perched near my shoulder. Something cold touched my neck. I resisted the urge to look as Robert had warned. He'd said under any type of observation, your eyes reveal pupil dilation and could be perceived as aggression. At the time, he'd thought I'd face human examination, not mechanical. Still, I applied the same caution.

I tried to breathe deeply, but the tension in the repugnant atmosphere made me draw air in gasps. My mental calendar kicked in as I realized...the final purchase order for my bridal bouquet and altar flower selection was due at nine this morning. Eva would be upset over my no-show. She'd think it was the same reason I cancelled an appointment last week—urgent delivery for a VIP customer. Only this time, she'd be wrong. An ill-timed chuckle escaped my pressed lips. She wouldn't believe where I was stuck if I told her!

My home in Silver Stone felt a world away. Robert, even farther.

Apart, but together, my words to Eva crept into my mind. Tears flooded my eyes as our last conversation swept my thoughts. Lying on this chilly ground, with a fake metal bird now perched on my shoulder was surreal, regrettable even. But someone asked me here to Snowy Peaks. I wasn't here on my own, and I was yet to meet him. I wiped my eyes clear, fresh determination taking over.

Lived in Maryland my entire life and never heard of this place. The mayor had sent an SOS. Asked me to come. Said Pete Zendel had bought the town through an auction and had forcefully taken it over.

I thought it was a joke. Zendel was in prison, locked away, forgotten. I testified at his trial ten months ago, watched him being led away after the verdict. No way he could buy *anything* from prison. Then I saw the photos, proof of his purchase of the town, taken days earlier, as the date-and-time stamps revealed.

The mayor's message detailed how Snowy Peaks held an annual honorary auction online to celebrate the town's rich history and their founders' legacy of freedom. They gave former residents who now lived afar the opportunity to participate online, made admission free and open to all, and symbolically placed the town's worth at 920,000 dollars—a thousand representing each citizen of Snowy Peaks. Soon after bidding began, Pete Zendel somehow gained access to the auction from prison, placed an exact bid, and paid the full sum. Then he later claimed new ownership of the town. He'd paid online via an anonymous spending account. When they investigated his payment source, their investigation turned up empty, leaving them at his mercy.

The mayor noted he'd explained in response to an e-mail notice from Zendel—their town was not for sale. Period. If it were, it was certainly worth a lot more than 920,000 dollars. He'd further offered to refund the cost because the auction was simply symbolic, always had been. Zendel insisted the transaction was officially documented and therefore legal and binding on both parties. Making things worse, couple of days later, his lawyer showed up at Snowy Peaks to claim territory. Fed up, the mayor chose to reach out to me for help. He said my past triumphant experience with the man strengthened the basis for his decision.

So why did his message say nothing of the crickets? Maybe they weren't here then? I shook off the distraction. More crickets now hovered above the ones dancing in our faces.

Frankly, I believed such plotting existed well within Zendel's high-tech and crooked nature. I proceeded to research the town on the internet at the Silver Stone library—for abundance of caution. Most of its information, save old town images dating back thirty years, were marked Unavailable from search

engines. The fact that the town's main website—
www.snowypeakstown.com—showed "down for
construction" splashed across its welcome screen,
spiked my suspicion. Was someone trying to rewrite
the town's history? I alerted Robert, but he was more
concerned about me. He worried for my safety and
preferred to focus on our upcoming wedding. With
preparations at high gear and our wedding only two
weeks away, we'd need to put *everything* on hold if I
accepted the request to go to Snowy Peaks. My business could grind to a screeching halt. Our lives could
stop. For Zendel—again.

Robert wanted to go in my stead, but I'd volun-
teered. The mayor knew of him yet asked for me.
There had to be a reason. Moreover, I thought I could
get away more easily if things got rough, being a
woman. Robert may not, being a cop. I wasn't willing
to let him intentionally embrace danger for my sake
again. Not after Zendel's failed attempt to kill Robert
when Zendel held me hostage months ago. I'd
chosen, never again.

Robert then insisted Charlie and others from his
unit—these four men—accompanied me, with the
approval of his captain, the police chief. The captain
initially wanted to send a full force squad with me,
but later agreed to keep things low-key until I
returned with on-the-ground details. In his words, "If
I don't hear from you in three days, we'll storm Snowy
Peaks."

Today was day two.

~

C HAPTER TWO
A cold blue-tipped beak pinched my
arm, and I squealed, glaring at the cricket as
it straightened. *Heart Rate-80 bpm* flashed on its
oblong belly fitted with a screen, followed by Normal
then a beep as the square screen went blank. But my
heart raced wildly. *Can't be true!* When I could feel the
blood thumping in my ears—fast. Unless Robert's
device in my ear threw off its rhythm? Many workings
of that tiny black button! I'd asked him for details; he
said there was no time to explain. Just put it on. I did.

The hovering cricket lifted and flew skyward,
whisking away. So did those observing the men. A
collective sigh of relief was in order as creaky wings
rose higher, sounded farther. I swung my head toward
Charlie, and the smile, which had begun to stretch my
face, dried. His weapon now out, was trained up the
sky, eyes squinting as he scrambled to his feet. The
other men rose too, aimed high, and began to shoot as
though they received an unspoken order.

"Charlie! Stop!" Too late.

Arrhythmic gunfire rang out. Sounded like a clash
of metal when they began hitting their intended
target high up. I swallowed. This time clutched by fear
and not tension. Why couldn't we gratefully leave in
peace?

I sprang to my feet and depressed my hand on my
bulletproof vest to steady myself. Then I rushed
toward Charlie, whose eyes stayed trained to the sky. I

balanced against the pillar separating us. He didn't stop shooting. Vibrations flowed from his active weapon and visibly shook his clothing. As I gripped the back of his jacket, the agitation crawled up my legs and shook me from feet first.

Desperate, I sprawled to the ground behind him and tugged at his vest. I wished for him to cease, but stayed out of the line of fire.

"Charlie!" I remembered his wife, Chrissy, and his son, Jaden—turning five in a couple of months. He had to remember them. Someone had to remind him.

A piercing sound hit him, and he staggered back, sank to his knees, and then to the ground. He was hit on his chest, close to his lungs. As I kneeled beside him, he clutched a piece of his jacket with his free hand. His weapon slid down his arm, then rested against his chin. Blood dripped out one corner of his mouth.

I held his head on my chest, so it didn't hit the ground. The rapid fire of the other weapons stopped, almost at the same time. All fell silent. Only my erratic breathing filled my ears, Charlie borne on my arms.

I uttered a guttural cry, grabbed his vest, and shook him vigorously. "Charlie!"

He gripped my arm. "Ruby, no way out town." His grip weakened. Then his hand dropped to the ground.

"Help! Somebody, help me!" I pressed a hand to where I'd seen spotting, fighting to stop his blood loss.

Soon, armed men emerged, weapons raised, all

trotting toward me. The crickets flew down, returned, and hovered frantically.

I spat out to the ground. They killed my team. The crickets' bellies—now opened fully—exposed a hidden weapon cavity that I didn't see the first time around. If only Charlie had suspected...

Two of the men in black fatigues, wearing military-grade black boots, stomped closer and trained their weapons on me. The rest waited, armed and ready. So did the crickets. One glance at each of their exposed belly cavities, jutting forward what could only be a weapon, confirmed my earlier fears. They weren't built only to observe and report. They were armed—and dangerous. A winged army.

I glared at both men and machines. Enticed to confront, but it would be pointless. I was out-manned, out-machined, and outgunned. Stuck in a place with no way out as Charlie last said. I gritted my teeth at the memory of him.

Cornered, I raised my hands in surrender, eyes pinned down on Charlie's unmoving body. Why did he have to? Hot tears tore through my lids. Rising, my eyes crossed over to the other three, where they also lay still. Gone. Bravest men I'd ever met. I swallowed, grief bubbling into quiet sobs as three armed men drew closer, tied my hands back with strings, then pulled me forward by my vest while the crickets swirled overhead and followed.

The tall uncut grasses on the lawn opposite almost fully covered us. There were no witnesses. None could see this far off the road. As they led me away, crumbled pieces of my heart stayed behind, laying there with the friends I'd lost.

Facing more men in dark military fatigues ahead, with the crickets stubbornly circling above, knocked home two realities. First, this was too sophisticated for Zendel to be working alone. There had to be another party. Problem was, that other party seemed less calculating, more dangerous, and killed without reckon. Second, I was alone in Snowy Peaks. Only God could help me now. *Oh, God, our help in ages past...* The age-old song began in my heart.

~

Forty-Eight Hours Earlier...
"You're late."

I strode briskly to the reception desk, smiled at the bob hair-styled, bright-smiling associate manning it. She thumbed down the list to my name then checked me in electronically into my appointment. "Did I really need an appointment for wedding nails, Eva? Plus I'm only a couple of minutes behind," I responded without looking.

"Thank you," I said to the associate. She smiled in response as I spun to face her boss.

Eva—owner of T.I.S.H. Bridals on Sycamore Street, Silver Stone—tall, classy, and with a build like a supermodel, glanced at the watch on her slender wrist. Only the measuring tape strung over her shoulder made her appear more a fashion designer. Her lime-green nail polish glistened off her fingers. "Half hour behind. Why an appointment? You've never seen a bride throw a fit over an ill-matched nail polish because it was off by a light color shade."

I grabbed my phone which I'd put down to check in. I'd forgotten to check in once before, and I got a call two days later about the missed appointment. Since moving to the central part of town, keeping these wedding prep appointments got a little more convenient. Though I missed my former neighbors—they being my very first business clients—my commute became faster between my office and everywhere I typically needed to be. But not today. "Blame it on 95 traffic."

She frowned, rejecting an incoming call on her phone as she drew closer. "You took 95 North at noon on a *Friday*?" She waved a dismissive hand, hugged me lightly. "Okay, you're early then." We both laughed. "It's good to see you again, my favorite June bride-to-be."

I chuckled. "Been almost one year, and I'm still getting used to the title. Almost as strange as hearing Robert call me 'my heartbeat'. I love it, but it will take some getting used to. I'm used to being called Ruby."

She arched a brow. "And *Red*. I heard him call you Red twice during your first appointment."

I smiled, recalling how self-conscious he was by being surrounded by rows of wedding dresses and squealing, excited brides. "Yes, Red. He's called me Red so long I might as well tag it on as a middle name."

Her shoulders shook with laughter as she waved me further down the line of testing rooms. I followed close, noting other brides-to-be chatting with bridal consultants in smaller meeting and fitting rooms.

Her bridal consultants took notes with hurried fingers, snapped photos of memorabilia that clients brought with them, and checked and confirmed wedding dress options with brides. The place was a bevy of activity, no doubt. And Eva was the best. She nailed customer service to a *T*. A bride tested a swirly milk-white dress, glancing at me. She looked stunning, and the lace design, which swept from her midsection to the sides, flaunted her feminine shape. When she locked gaze with me, I stopped.

"You like?" Her eyes appeared unsure.

I hesitated, wary to give advice on something as important as a wedding dress. "The top gives you full coverage so you don't have to worry about bending. The waist shows your trim figure and flows to the swirly trail. You look lovely. Yes, I like." My honest assessment.

Eva prodded my arm with a gentle tug, and I moved along. Rows of wedding dresses in display hangers lined the white-splashed wall on the side. Something about seeing them again lured a smile to my face. I liked wedding dresses, even as a little girl, though I rarely saw one up close. Low overhead lighting spotted each and made them captivating. I glanced away, focused on Eva. Good thing I'd already chosen my wedding dress. It was perfect for me.

Sliding past decorative milk-white silk curtains

flowing down a window near the end of the display lounge, I let Eva usher me into a wide room with four lounge chairs. Two sat at the far corners while two others faced each other, and a chandelier hung at the center. An open window lodged between both chairs, giving the area a homey feel. I felt welcome.

"Let me get the test colors for you. We have a wide array. I'll be right back." Her poised frame disappeared into a narrow office by the right, leaving me to admire the room's exquisite décor. A waist-length gold-encrusted mirror hung on the wall above a two-seat sofa, next to an open window. Parted curtains fluttered as breeze blew in softly. I walked toward it and sat. Initially she'd advised that natural lighting revealed color tones better than indoor ones.

Eva emerged minutes later rolling a pink-colored, four-tiered box cart. She wheeled it to a stop near my feet. Color palette labels affixed on its sides for each tier. Pressing a button at the uppermost tier, she released the latch, and it flew open, revealing a vibrant display of color assortment.

"Wow! All these *just* for nails?"

She drew a seat close. "You can't imagine how important your nail polish is."

"Why?"

"Because everyone will stare at your fingers when he places the ring there. It's next in importance to the wedding dress and earrings in my opinion, and in that order."

She took my hand, cast by the natural sunshine glow streaming in the window. "I do this with all my brides. The color of your nails could spark pleasant memories of your groom on your wedding day. That's what we want to do." She rested my left hand flat on the armrest. "Tell me, Ruby, what is your warmest memory of Robert? As far back as you can recall."

I exhaled long and sighed. Wasn't hard. Closing my eyes, I relaxed into the plush chair. "We were ten. The orphanage took us to a picnic. We'd all been so excited and waited for it like for Christmas morning. For a bunch of kids, orphans no one particularly cared about, we felt special getting a fun day in town."

I stretched my feet beneath a table where a happy bride smiled from the cover of *Eastern Wedding Digest*. "There was going to be lots of cotton candy, chocolate cake, and soda." Even now, my mouth watered. "We were thrilled. That day, all the kids filed into the park. As usual, Robert was in the circle of his guy friends, while I sat with my girl friends on low-cut green grass opposite them at Fenway Park."

I opened my eyes and saw hers growing misty. I sat up, then snapped my feet back, and looked ahead. "Midway through the feast and belly full, for some reason I began searching for him. Our eyes met across the meadow, surrounded by colorful flowers, and he smiled broadly, acknowledging me. I still recall, I wore a bright pink flay dress. In that moment, it was almost as if, though apart, we were together. Still looked out for each other across the distance." I chuckled and turned to her, my smile lingering. "That would be my warmest memory."

"Apart, but together," she repeated. "That is so touching! Thank you for sharing."

Her eyes watered more, and she swiped a tear. "Based on that." She reached into the first tiered box and rattled a couple of tall nail lacquer bottles. She lifted one, smiling. "I've chosen the perfect color— whitish pink or as we call it, Bride Shine. It's got a cream-white color base overcast with a light pink shade, with a slight tint to make it pop." She rose and ushered me to the nail station near her office. "C'mon. Let's go try it on you and see how it looks."

I obliged, rose too. As I followed her, I recalled what the sweet memory I just related had prodded afresh to the fore of my mind, and I chuckled again. *Apart, but together.*

$\sim$

CHAPTER THREE
ROBERT

"Shuffling through paperwork is my least favorite task, Charlie."

Charlie threw his head back and roared with laughter, and then pointed a finger. "I'm not the sergeant. You are. Now, you choose whether you like sitting in your air-conditioned office," he pointed at the window, "or out there in the sweltering heat running street patrol."

My eyes shot up. "Right." Hated to admit it, but he had a point. Out there, thanks to the late spring weather, it was steaming hot in the afternoons while trying to keep impatient drivers from butting car heads. In here, air-conditioning made report writing less tedious. Something about telling how my workday went wearied me, unless it was to Ruby. I'd rather show it.

"There's an incentive though." The wink as he rubbed his jaw could spell a "very good" thought or mischief.

"Um, what, Charlie? No, I'm not going to sit here to have take-out for lunch third time this week so you can watch the Titan's basketball game—again," I said flatly.

He ignored my sully mood. "That's not what I was going to say!"

The drop in his excitement told me it was what he would've wanted. I tossed my completed report sheet on top of this week's growing pile. "What were you saying then?"

He broke into a smile and leaned out his chair. "I saw Ruby this morning, off Saddlebury Lane at the coffee shop."

I glanced up. "Really?" She'd told me she had an appointment soon, so why go out of her way?

"She was entering as I came out. Anyway, she mentioned she'd gotten an urgent delivery request from a regular client, but all her staff were out, so she took the delivery herself."

I pressed my lips and turned toward the computer

so Charlie wouldn't see my displeasure. I'd warned her to stay off the street after her experience with Zendel. To ensure her safety in case he came after her again. She'd hired more staff for this very purpose. I exhaled, pushing it off my mind.

Charlie continued, "She'd hinted that she had a bridal appointment afterward at lunchtime at T.I.S.H." His smile grew wider. "Then she asked if I'd seen you this morning."

I drummed my fingers on the desk. Charlie tended to ramble when he let loose. On the battlefield, he was a machine, rarely talked and always focused on the mission. Like two sides of a coin—two very different sides.

"Yes, she told me about it when I asked her about our lunch plans."

He waved, intolerant with my interruption and probably irritated over being rushed along. "I thought, since you know where she is at the moment, why don't you surprise her for lunch? You know, drive down, make a splash welcome, and sweep her off to a loving lunch. What do ya think? Mind you, in two weeks, you'll both be eating from the same dish."

His reference to our wedding didn't escape me. I'd been counting the days. He did have a point. I could surprise her... A smile curved my lips.

～

RUBY
I raised my left hand to the light, examining Bridal Shine on my fingers. "Perfect! I like it."

Eva pointed to the technician who'd done it. "Would you please return these to the office? Oh, and grab my camera from my desk on your way back. I need to take a snap of these gorgeous nails for our records."

I blew softly on my glistening nails, now almost dried, wishing the color didn't have to come off soon. Moments later, I angled my hand on the design table, and Eva snapped multiple shots of my nails. I observed it more, noting its allure, pondering how she got the perfect nail color for me simply from a story. "Amazing. This color mix is like..." I pondered the right word, shifting my fingers in perspective beneath the light.

"Bubblegum. Dipped in white chocolate. Love it. And love you." A soft hand on my back and a kiss on my forehead followed the masculine rumble of words.

I raised my head, jumped to my feet, and then sprang into his arms. "Robert! What are you doing here?" I reached over and smacked Charlie's arm. "I know. You led him here."

Charlie winked, and they exchanged a knowing glance.

I pressed Robert's cheeks playfully. "Did you miss me that much, or were you bored with paperwork? I know how much you 'enjoy' those."

He broke into a smile. His eyes brilliantly bore into mine. "Both."

We stayed in a loose hug as he glanced at Eva behind Charlie. "Hi, Eva. Sorry for cutting into your appointment. I missed her."

She nodded and gave an understanding smile. "No need to apologize, Robert. Grooms are welcome at T.I.S.H. Bridals, as are the brides. You just can't see her in her wedding dress yet." Serving him a mischievous wink, she touched my shoulder. "We should be done now. The technician will wipe the colors off your nails, and you're free to go. It seems someone needs you more than I do." She waved at Robert, turned, and strode toward her office where I'd seen her next client waiting.

He swept me into a full embrace, leaned in, and whispered, "Thirteen days, love. Until we're married. So excited."

I chuckled, and then pulled back a little. "I know. Unbelievable, right? God is good." How new this entire experience had been at first. It had felt quite different from best friends, morphing into betrotheds. It didn't feel weird, just...unique, like we could talk about more intimate details of our lives without it sounding odd. We had complete trust because we'd already seen the best and worst of ourselves while keeping our clothes on. Of course, neither of us was perfect. We knew that. There were days we couldn't stand each other, days we fought over little things not worthy of a second thought. Or we simply needed alone time. But at the end of the day, we'd get back to each other, and most times, even laughed it off and wondered why we disagreed. On more serious issues, we talked it through. We were in this for the rest of our lives. We'd stay married to each other and make it work, God helping us. That was our firm decision.

He lifted my purse from the table, guided me as we walked toward the door, Charlie trailing. When we neared the door, I took my purse from him, unzipped it, searching for my car keys. Then he peeked inside, grabbed something, and winked.

I knew what it was. I raced him for it as he fled through the doors. I noticed he appeared sharp even in uniform. "Robert, please don't eat it!"

He already tore off a piece from my coveted *Armour* sweetened raw dark chocolate and tossed it in his mouth, laughing. "I'm hungry."

I mock-punched his arm. "Robert! I was saving that for a snack."

He held it out. "I split it in two. See." He fed the leftover half-piece in my mouth. I observed his well-manicured hands, smiling as I sucked in the chocolate.

He tossed the wrapper in a nearby dumpster as we approached the parking. Then he stopped. "Wanna have lunch, Red? That way, you won't need the chocolate replaced." A broad grin lit his face.

I scowled. "If that's supposed to make me feel better, well... it did. Let's go, emerald eyes."

He curled a hand around my waist as we reached their ride, Robert's car. He handed Charlie the keys.

Charlie pushed a button and flicked the car

unlocked. "Okay, lovebirds, you take the back seat while I drive. Hopefully, O'Malleys should be free of lunch crowds now, and we can grab a group table."

When we arrived at O'Malleys a half hour later, Charlie's hope was met. The open grill at the middle of the restaurant, which typically saw larger crowds during lunch, was scanty now with only three patrons in queue. A couple of single tables were occupied. However, larger group tables sat mostly empty. We chose a spot close to the door. Robert preferred having visibility of entrances and exits. Charlie did too. Must have to do with them being cops.

"Sweet onion rings on grilled chicken. Rice and lima beans tomato stew. Oh, and some lime juice. Thanks." I gave the waiter my order.

Robert turned, picking free bread from the basket on our table. "No strawberries today?"

I liked the bread, but didn't take one. I shook my head. "Nope. Trying to get in shape for our wedding." I winked.

He laughed then put the bread back. "All right then. I'll have what she's having. Trying to get in shape too. I'm not coming in with a huge tummy. Add an apple, please." The waiter took notes.

Charlie nodded to the waiter. "I need double the size of whatever they're having. Seriously. This man has not eaten in a while." He pointed to his stomach, frowning.

When we laughed at his humor, he shrugged. "I'm not trying to get in shape for anything. And I'm already married. Might as well eat up."

Robert raised a hand. "Whoa, take it easy. You're the best man, remember? I'd hate to see you fall asleep on us at the altar, buddy."

Charlie waved it off. "Who said anything about falling asleep? Just trying to eat for three." We all burst out laughing as our meals streamed in moments later, served along with free soda drinks, which I skipped.

I pointed my fork at his stacked plate. "That's right, Charlie. Eat up. Only someone who didn't know you worked out two hours at the gym every day would be fooled by your zealous eating habit."

Lunch was over within an hour, and Charlie headed out first. Said he needed to pick up something for his son, Jaden, before returning to the station. Robert and I stayed back for a bit to discuss some wedding prep.

My phone rang. "It's an unknown number." I glanced from the phone to Robert.

He frowned. "Go ahead. Answer it."

I pressed Accept.

"Hello?" A voice began. "Hello. This message is for Ruby Masters, in care of Robert Towers. This is an SOS message from the mayor of Snowy Peaks. Pete Zendel has seized our town. We need your help. This message is private and cannot be shared publicly or I could lose my life. Please help us."

I lowered the phone, upon hearing the name, Zendel. I gaped at Robert. My eyes felt rounded, and my mouth dropped open.

END OF SAMPLE.

Get your next book SNOWY PEAKS now.
Link: https://books2read.com/u/mlvXPb
Thank you for reading.

~

Join my VIP readers club and never miss a sale, giveaway or new release: http://www. joyohagwu.com/announcements.html

~

YOUR NEW BEGINNING STARTS NOW, NO MORE DELAY, FRIEND.
    You can start a new beginning with GOD. [I capitalize GOD for respect, a personal choice].
    Please pray this prayer today and watch your life transform beyond your imagination!:
    GOD, I come to YOU in the Name of JESUS. I am a sinner and have fallen short of your glory. I believe JESUS is the Son of GOD. I believe that YOU sent YOUR Only Begotten Son JESUS CHRIST to die and pay the price for my sins. I believe HE died, rose from the dead on the third day and is seated at the right Hand of GOD. I choose to accept Jesus Christ as my personal LORD and Savior. I accept the forgiveness of my sins. And I receive GOD's gift of everlasting life with GOD. Please give me YOUR HOLY SPIRIT forever to live inside me. I am born again. Thank YOU GOD for saving me. May I see YOUR Hand at work in

my life starting now, so much I give YOU all the glory right now. In JESUS CHRIST Most powerful name amen.

CONGRATULATIONS! Welcome to the family of GOD. My life transformed for good when I said this prayer. This is the first step. Step into your new life.

Please click below if you said this prayer for the first time. I have a free gift for you.

https://landing.mailerlite.com/webforms/landing/e0x9v7

GOD bless you.

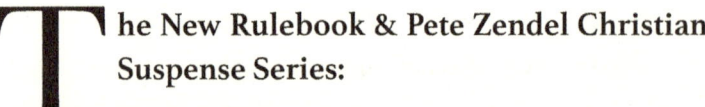

The New Rulebook & Pete Zendel Christian Suspense Series:

- Book 12 : Hunter
- Book 13 : Hunted
- Book 14 : Courageous
- Book 15 : Defended
- Book 16 : Warrior
- Book 17 : Emergent
- Book 18 : Reign
- Book 19 : Legacy
- Book 20 : Emergent

Made in the USA
Monee, IL
04 April 2022